FRAME BY FRAME:

Justice Served

By

Mathews

Nkoboli

Lehlongwane

III

CONTENTS

Dedication

I dedicate this work to my Creator, Guide and Guardian. I always remain in awe as to how He has kept this talent alive in me. I sometimes want to shed it for something else but at almost every turn, I will be reminded of what I knack I have for telling stories.

I especially dedicate this book to fathers; it is no easy task teaching children how not to be you, more so when you have seen the errors of your ways and to redirect yours and your children's life skills education in this trying and volatile era.It is not to say that mothers have it any easier, particularly single mother, so please also accept my words as I pass on by and place urgency to fathers.

My foundations, pillars and rocks: Lady Bishop Lehlongwane (Mum), Ms Ngcobo (Mum Thelma), Mrs. Lehlongwane (Caramel) and Mr and Mrs. Mlonzi (Marks and Sarah). Your parts in shaping these stories have been far too invaluable.

I markedly dedicate this to my stabilisers, near and far; my children. Honestly I think I would have made some even dafter decisions if you weren't in my life. You are literally the real life translation of "What would Jesus do!?!" except my version is "What would my kids say and how do I expect to guide them to be their best if this is the example I'm putting out there?" Okay, it doesn't always work but practice makes perfect!

To the readers that keep this ancient craft alive, you have got to be the most important aspect of this entire cycle. It is absolutely amazing to conceive and write a tale but to have it read by countless people and have them keep the story alive, is beyond any scope and magnitude imaginable.

Foreword

What sad yet interesting times we live in. We live in a world where crime and evil have become such daily occurrences as breathing or adherence to the laws of self-preservation.

Primarily, if a person is not or doesn't have some sort of criminal tendency in them, they are actually the real threat to today's society. For instance, if a person drives to and keeps to the road laws they are more likely to be treated as a road nuisance and they would face the wrath and rage of other road users, especially taxi drivers. The other 21st Century phenomenon is the viral photography; we have become so obsessed with being popular or being the first to share the photography that we have forgotten how to physically save lives.

How did we allow ourselves to degenerate to such low levels? It's quite simple really; we kept on pushing the morality levels further and further away, turning a blind eye and fooling ourselves that accepting that times are changing and that we have to keep up. We justified and quantified to make our actions more palpable and acceptable. In short we lied to ourselves that what we were doing was okay and if it somehow seemed less than okay then our egos took over until we became indifferent. However, deep down we knew and always know that wrong is wrong and no amount of justification would change that.

We created buzz words and catch phrases to make ourselves feel better about the wrongs that we have committed and we definitely knew that it was wrong because more than anything or having to be told by someone else, our bodies just have a natural tendency of rejecting anything that is wrong.

An indication that something we've done is off the mark is when we have an inexplicable urge to cough it out to someone, sometimes almost as a brag and a dare. This in itself is a clear sign that our being is rejecting that which we have done; hence the saying: 'It doesn't go down well with me.' Another sign, one that actually attests to our being's rejection of malady is the actual physical sickness that we experience, ranging from thirst all the way to excretion. Yet somehow, we find a way to push beyond that barrier and push the envelope until morality is a blip in our rear view mirror and from there on we seek companionship in this abyss because after all humans are social not solitary beings and that gives rise to: 'The more, the merrier!'

We ask how we have allowed for our moral fibre to be so corrupted. We went with the flow that's how; we took the easy path and didn't want to stay on the moral high ground. We refuse to rehabilitate ourselves and lead by good example; we find loopholes to exploit instead of patching them up. Some people have become so skilled at being apathetic in terms of morality that syndication was just the most natural next level for them; an evolution of sorts.

The worst backlash of this slippery road is that the majority of society that still conform to morality pay the price through tougher laws that are meant to catch out the criminals, laws like RICA and FICA, gradually the State becomes a nanny or a Big Brother state.

It may all seem bleak and like doom and gloom but actually there is hope and there is a way out: stay the course, stay strong and keep the faith. For every person that you affect positively, is one less person falling into the void; every good example that you set is a mustard seed sown to bloom. You are not a person of instant gratification that is why it is not so easy to corrupt you.

As you venture into the words and pages of this book, place this social media quote in your mind.

"WHAT BEGINNING

I SOMETIMES ASK MYSELF WHY GOOD PEOPLE ARE BEING TREATED SO UNFAIRLY, I'VE SEEN GOOD MEN AND WOMEN WHO STRIVE TO SEE THE GOOD IN PEOPLE BUT IN RETURN THEY HAVE HAD THEIR EFFORTS GET THROWN BACK INTO THEIR FACES. WE DO HAVE WOMEN OF SUBSTANCE OUT THERE AND WE HAVE GOD FEARING MEN OUT THERE. NO MATTER HOW HARD IT HURTS, BELIEVE YOU ME I KNOW, DON'T GET DISCOURAGED, CONTINUE DOING GOOD, I KNOW IT TOOK YOU YEARS TO BUILD THAT RELATIONSHIP, BUT SOMEONE BROKE IT IN A SECOND, I KNOW HOW PAINFUL IT IS TO DO THINGS AND THEN BEING TOLD "THAT'S NOT GOOD ENOUGH", BUT WHAT IS IMPORTANT IS THAT WE MUST STOP FEELING SORRY FOR OURSELF, INSTEAD WE DUST IT OFF AND CONTINUE DOING WHAT WE'RE BEST AT...GOD IS LOVE..."

SELLO MOGAPI

THE PATSY

The sleepless nights continued, at times with a minimum of two nightmares per night, followed by cold sweats and feelings of asphyxia and gasping for air. Sometimes the nightmares would be so violent that I would be woken up by the physical pain caused by involuntarily punching the bedside stand. The meditation and self-medication was having little to no effect and I would find myself seriously craving a hard drink just so that I could pass out and pass out heavily at that. I was being eaten up by a number of issues and there was not even one shrink that could help me get out of the vortex. It surely wasn't from a lack of trying, it was just that his system was over-loading and it was clearly showing signs of wearing out. It was bad enough dealing with the nocturnal activities but then the diurnal ones were not much of a consolation either. At a certain point I was close to being a zombie and truly felt like a basket case, where the world's worst scenarios had just been dumped in and then there were days when I would be catatonic, where I would sit and just gaze aimlessly into the open and then without warning shriek back to reality.

I could not understand why having done the right thing, or so I thought, brought me so much grief, pain and angst. I began to think that they, society, had lied to me when they said that in doing the right thing I would feel better and that I would be a better person and, of course, that I would be an acceptable and respectable member of society. I believed them, I had to believe them, and after all I was brought up on a good moral code and a great set of values. My parents were prominent and respected members of the community, as were their parents; so it was improbable and highly unlikely that I got bad rearing from home. I had a strong religious upbringing, so strong that our house was built right next to the church along with the late Archbishop Masango's daughters' houses but ours was the only one that was directly across his bedroom window. Furthermore, I had been privileged enough to attend a great catholic school in the plush northern suburbs of Jozi, during the apartheid era for that matter. I was, for the greatest part of those years, treated with dignity by both adults and children alike, which in turn taught me that regardless of their disposition a person deserved to be respected. It was thus engrained in my world that if something was good, it was good and if it was bad then it was bad; it was as simple as that, there was no gray or questionable area about such things and such things did not require a jury. I was taught what was good and what was bad and at all times, I was encouraged to be good to such an extent that during my high school years, one of the brothers of the La Salle order actually asked me if I would not consider joining the order. I declined on the basis that I looked forward to having copious amounts of sex as I grew up (I had actually contemplated the notion of being a porn star) and their franchise and line of work would not allow for me to pursue that career.

Even without too much effort, the events that took place that morbid morning got played out in slow motion in my mind and I would visualise how that band of faux lawmen plotted their raid and their options from the onset. I pondered whether when they left their homes and loved ones had they kissed them goodbye, as Nthabi and I always did when we parted? Did they wish their kids well and tell them that they loved them and wish God's blessing upon them when they dropped them off at school, as we always had done with our children? What had they been doing the night before the raid? Did they enjoy a meal with their family and talk to each other about the day's events? How did they get duped into this, were they told that it would be a career boosting move or was it something that they did so often that it had eventually corroded their conscience? I wondered to myself how they psyched themselves up for that type of operation. Did they use their own drugs or alcohol or did they just need a pep talk? Did they sit in the same room as they would have sat in for a legal bust and as with a legal bust, did they place all the investigation's pictures and notes up on their notice boards so that they had my paper life mapped for everyone to see? Did they even do a proper investigation on me or was it some hasty botch up right from the start? Had they ever even laid eyes on me before that day or was that all part of their charade? How much did they earn for that bust? How long did that money last them? Was it really worth it? Did they sleep easy that night, knowing that they had wrongfully and maliciously arrested an innocent man and helped another in ruining mine? Did they even care? Who were these men really? All these questions demanded answers and I was not getting any and with each unanswered question, I was slowly slipping into another realm, a dark and murky realm where my thoughts were less than forgiving to my conspirators and my imagination had a lot to offer. I realised then that there seems to be a vault in our minds where we can make multiple withdrawals from our darker side and all these withdrawals were all interest free. After some time I had little else to think of because I didn't want to think of anything else. I was bitter and angry; angrier than before this whole thing started.

I had started on this matter with the intention to correct the injustices done to me and if the people that had the power vested in them were not willing to help then I would have to be the one to finish what I had started. After all, my family motto is: 'if it's worth doing then its worth doing well' and this task was not completed.

My conspirators pegged me to be a law abiding citizen, one whom they had figured that they would just take liberties with and they were right but they failed to thoroughly check where this supposedly gullible and naive person came from. It is true that I came from a good and respectable family but where I grew up, respect was not a take out meal that was just ordered and delivered to one's lap; it had to be earned and sometimes through hard measures and sometimes unscrupulous means. There are some things that I could never unlearn, no matter what ever else I did; they would forever remain entrenched in my being. I suppose that was one of the reasons why my father made sure that I went to a good catholic school instead of the township school which was within walking distance from home. He, like any concerned parent was hoping that I would not get swayed into an unsavoury lifestyle; one that he and his brothers had seen and were surrounded by, a lifestyle where the law was in a person's own hands. Then again the law of the land at that time did not really do much to protect the township citizen; it merely kept them at bay; in the township to be precise. Labour laws were there but not in their favour, the same could be said for various other statutes. The one law that was enforced, if and when the perpetrator was caught, was capital punishment. Oh, there were plenty hangings during my parents' heyday but even that was jaded. A case of assault wouldn't receive so much attention but a killing would definitely end up with a hanging or life imprisonment if the perp was lucky. So it was common, if not acceptable to beat the daylight out of someone who spat at you or looked at you funny but just as long as that person wasn't killed. Those were the days of an eye for an eye, a tooth for a tooth.

I have seen people being beaten up to the point that the ground was the colour of their blood and they were the colour of the ground. One of my uncles once struck a guy so viciously with his left that the poor bloke cracked the concrete paving when he fell and another uncle, who under normal circumstances was a very sweet man, had a kick of a mule. I suppose his legs had been strengthened by the endless hours of Wu Shu training; he shattered an opponent's shin. The one uncle that amazed me the most was the one who always attacked the torso and he knew exactly how to knock the wind out of an opponent before they could even get a chance to draw their fist back to strike. My father was as skilled a martial artist as he was a cowboy; a real arms fanatic. He spent whatever spare time he had either in the dojo or on the shooting range and he was exceptionally good at both. He also insisted that my sisters and I received the proper firearms training because he felt that once we knew how to handle firearms we would be better equipped, legally and otherwise. In an unorthodox way, he was right; we knew the dangers and repercussions of discharging a firearm at any point in time and we were also quite well versed with the various firearm legislations, heck we knew those laws even better than average policeman. I strongly believe that it was also through that gun training and practice that I became more skilful in reasoning out situations. You see once a gun is unholstered and in the hand, during a fight or altercation, no matter how trivial; you are the one who has authority and power. The one who is looking down the barrel has very little to say, if anything at all and should any emotions not be in check then the situation is bound to spiral out of control. Sadly, once a round has been fired, it can never be recalled; so the best thing is to keep the gun holstered or not to carry it at all. Furthermore, there's no predicting what the other person will do when they see the gun; they might not get scared but rather fight and that usually ends up with a fatality. So it's not the gun that is a problem; it's the person on the trigger end that is the problem.

My father and my uncles with all that capability to inflict pain on others always emphasised that violence solves nothing. They did their utmost to keep all their sons out of the violent arena and for some of us it worked but then there were some of us who were just our fathers' sons. The fight could not be taken out, no matter how hard they tried. Even though there were street brawls and shebeen fights; none of my cousins have lost their lives through violence, we have collected some battle ground scars and shed a few pints of blood but we always lived to tell the story at the next family gathering. In some instances we would go find the other guy and his posse and pay them back for the unscheduled trip to the hospital that they had arranged for our kinsman. It was the way of the township and that was exactly what our fathers did not want us to grow up with, they wanted us to grow to be decent, law abiding citizens and honourable men. They wanted us to be the men who would lend reason to unreasonable situations and leave great and noble legacies. Wimps! Far from it. They wanted a better life for us and they taught us to stand up for what we believed in and importantly to uphold the law. The way things were going we were supposed to be the better generation, the one that would foster peace and humanity. We were not going to grow up as thugs; not just for their sake but for ours and our children too. That is why they worked hard for us, teaching, coaching and mentoring us and even shedding their old ways and the truth is that my father succeeded. He raised me in a way that I am proud to be his son and in a way that I can unashamedly teach my sons to be the men and leaders of tomorrow.

This is why it pained me to do what I was about to do because I would be undoing my father's lifetime of hardwork and if only I could shield my children from it all, I gladly would. However, in my failure to act what would I be saying to them; that it fine to have people take advantage of you and do as they please with you, your freedom, your life and in the end all you should do is cower, lick your wounds and hope that it's over? If I chose not to do anything about that matter then why would I teach them our family motto or tell them to stand up for what they believe in or stand up for injustice? I might as well tell them to pack it in and forget about trying to live honest lives because the honest people don't get their just reward or the fact that if they try speak up against wrong then they themselves would fall prey to the injustice. No! I don't want to raise children that would have nothing to believe in or them not believing that I was a righteous father. If I didn't teach them how do the right thing or fight for the right thing and we, as parents, all don't teach our children that then we might as well look forward to a lawless society and accept that we are uncivilised and uncouth. Deep in my being I firmly believe that I did the right thing and facts and the law backed me up on that even though I unjustly treated at the end of it all. The men and women who failed to act within their perimeters of the authority needed to be exposed to the world for what they truly were. I sought justice, nay; I demanded that justice be served.

THE PAWNS

The objectives of the police service are to prevent, investigate crime thus combating it, they are also there to maintain public order, to protect and secure the people of the country and their property and to uphold and enforce the laws of the land. The men and women that are employed to render this service are carefully selected, screened and thoroughly trained in these and other facets to help them perform their tasks dutifully and professionally. The parliamentarians and law makers assure us that this process happens meticulously and as the public and citizens of a country, we then get a sense of comfort and security from knowing that our police services or any police force for that matter are good at what they are supposed to do. It is also from this knowledge and the indoctrination that we receive from the early stages in our lives that we are made to believe that anyone who has donned on a police uniform or uniform bearing such similarity is a good person but maybe we should have been taught that those people actually represent good. The same can be said when we see a person wearing a nurse's uniform or a person wearing a lab coat with a stethoscope hanging about on their neck. These are people who are there to do good and we are to trust them, though I must say I could never trust a bloke holding a needle telling me that it won't hurt. In general, they do not mean us any harm and they would not knowingly do so, except the doctor and his needle. However, the truth is that it's the institutions which they represent that seek to protect us or enhance our lives or rather; it's these institutions' rules and regulations that have the intent to do so. It's the people that are the issue and not the police service itself. People are just that people and being people they are prone to any and all mannerism of other people, regardless of the clothing they wear. For example, if the most senior of all police officers is the most corrupt in the organisation, the body of the organisation is bound to suffer the same malady. He would have clearly led by example. If he is protecting and serving a known and self confessed criminal then why would his subordinates protect and serve the ordinary citizen. Let's be honest, we all know someone in the police force and should we find ourselves in a spot of bother, we would make that call for them to come sort the mess out for us; sadly that's the society that we have become. In return, to show our gratitude, we would do them a favour which would be anything from buying them a drink or getting them an unapproved discount from our workplace. One hand washes the other as we all say but just how much of this communal hand washing is legal and justifiable and what will happen when this proverbial hand washing basin is completely dirty and full of gunge, who will then get the task of cleaning it out?

To get my plan in motion, I had to obtain as much information as I possibly could and with that though in mind I started off by skulking around the local police station, the very place where my sordid affair ended. Though it was in town and just off two very busy roads, I found that there were some quiet spots outside on the street where I could perch myself and watch the daily buzz around the place. At first it was from the comfort of my car but after two days, I realised that though the busy roads were providing a near perfect cover, a car was a rather prominent observation point which could easily be identified and with that I could be traced a lot quicker. Nonetheless those stakeout hours spent in that car were not in vain because from the safety and comfort of the car I was able to study and note the movements of the local PD (police department) and I got to see what time people got there for their shifts and what time they left after their shifts.

By all accounts, a police station is a hustle bustle of activity and there are very few moments when there is no activity at all. It all starts off at about 05h00 when a police bus drives in to the rear to drop off the morning shift change cops, they are there to relieve the ones that had been on duty throughout the night; though some members do make their own way to the station using their own form of transport, a number are bussed in. Fifteen minutes to half an hour later another bus or kombi load arrives with the some more members of the shift that would been picked up from further afield or from the barracks. Within ninety minutes after the drop off both the transport vehicles leave the station taking with them the off duty cops and one returns at about 07h30 with mostly ununiformed passengers, these are mostly the administrative personnel and thereafter the kombis remained parked until approximately 08h00 whereby they'll move out again with ununiformed passengers taking them to meetings or training. On their return, the empty kombis park for most of the day and they will start moving again at about 15h30, to go pick up the staff that had gone for training. Once that route has been completed, they then begin the transportation of the office staff at 16h30 and this usually takes up to four hours per kombi. At 17h00 another kombi or bus arrives to drop off the first main lot of the night shift cops and it then waits for the day shift bunch to hand over and sign off before it carts them off to their homes or drop off points.

The gumshoes usually seep into the scene from 07h30, for the supposedly diligent ones and their transport modes vary from their own trodden jalopies to the trodden Government Issue jalopies, though some are fortunate enough to pitch up in later models of the Government Issue jalopies. They seem to make cameo appearances at the PD because from about 09h00 they started leaving the hive again, usually in pairs but it was not always the case. For the rest of the day they drove in and out but mostly out. The brass then comes in at 08h00 and they are in somewhat acceptable vehicles, usually unmarked and they remain parked for the whole day until 16h30 or in the odd instance 17h30. The top brass only arrive after 09h00 in un-marked and plusher cars and they leave at about 16h00 or earlier, much earlier. The busiest of the lot at a police station are the patrol vans and cars; now this lot really burn fuel. They don't have a set time for entry or departure; they are just in and out, in and out, in and out the whole day. They are worse then worker bees in a hive. They also don't have a set driver; they are real communal cars. Anyone who has a licence and can get their keys to one can just pull out with a van and off they are to do their shopping or pick up a girlfriend or the occasional criminal or two.

In order for me to get closer to the people I went out and purchased some sweets, crisps, cigarettes packets and posed as a one-eyed, partly deaf, dreadlocked street vendor at one of their corners. That effectively gave me the opportunity to see, through my one good eye and a hidden camera and record material regarding the way they spoke to and about each other. I got a better insight into the way they rated and handled certain cases and how they inducted their cadets into the everyday operations. I was gob smacked when I heard on numerous occasions how the whole song and dance at the academy and the first parade addressed by the station commander was belittled and the cadets were urged to place little emphasis on those. The one senior, an inspector, who came by with his cadet to buy crisps was busy with his version of induction and he told the freshman to forget everything that he had ever learnt at the academy and what the station commander had said to him and the other newbies when they arrived at the station. He said that the law is written by a bunch of pencil pushers, who knew nothing about what really happens on the street. According to the seasoned veteran, most of the laws were airy fairy and far too constricting for them to do their job and too many to memorise, learn or even remember for them as the ordinary cop on the street and even if they knew them, the citizens would not even know that such laws existed. He said that according to him, the most important of these were the SAPS Act and the Criminal Procedures Act and even at that, they just needed to know bits and pieces of it really.

The most astonishing of all that he had said was that in a police officer's life the really important and most helpful thing that he would ever need was right there on his hip; his sidearm. He said that if he could not find a solution to any problem whatsoever, then the ultimate solution lay in the chamber of his 9mm service pistol. I felt a shudder as I thought of how many lives had been lost through service pistols, some being murder-suicides and others being results of the victim being at the wrong place at the wrong time. However this man was not done with his philosophy, he carried on, as he shoved another handful of crisps into his mouth, to say that the rookie should never see himself as being in the wrong in any situation because that would impair his judgement and should it be that he was wrong in a situation; when it came to crunch time he could always rely on the other cop who was with him to back him up but he should never openly admit guilt to anything. Confidently he continued to say that people, in general, do not know the laws and if they claim to do so then all they need to do, as the police, to soften this knowledgeable individual up, is to lock them up for a couple of hours on a minor charge like defeating the ends of justice or obstructing them from doing their job. He was adamant that in most cases when a person was charged and prosecuted on that charge, prosecutors and magistrates always had a sympathetic ear and the charge had never lost its weight in a court. According to him it was one of those charges that were there to scare public and once the matter got to the court it usually dragged on because the cop that lay the charge would go to the prosecutor the day before and ask for a postponement on the grounds that they were still investigating the matter. At times the matter would get postponed so many times that the court would finally strike it off the roll and dismiss the case completely, by then the accused has been thoroughly frustrated and if they took on the services of a lawyer then they would have paid a kings ransom but according to him the best part of all of that was that the cops would never get reprimanded for anything because it was highly unlikely that the accused would want to go near a court for an extremely long time. Further to that, civil matters tend to take even longer because they have to start off by reporting the matter to the station commander and when nothing comes about through that endeavour, the matter would then be taken to the ICD (Independent Complaints Directorate). The ICD, according to the inspector were a bunch of wet nurses that have never really got to know what the policing is like, they are mostly some snot-nosed, bureaucratic kids that hold some academic degree or diploma and would sooner be politicians than real cops. Months and even years later if and when the matter ends up in a civil court, most of them never even required the cop to appear in court as they are usually between the state and the individual, so by and large, it was a winning situation for the cops and they can remain a law unto themselves.

With that he crunched up the empty packet of crisps and threw it on the pavement and they left. In the time I spent there at the corner as a vendor, I also got a bonus on what they did for lunch or where they went for lunch and what were their usual meals and cravings were. Most cops liked pap and vleis and they would support the stalls at the taxi rank and railway station, which was where the cheapest and most heaped pap was served. That also explained why I had always seen a lot of patrol cars at the taxi rank.

A police station in itself is a grim place but generally abuzz, which makes it easier to observe but there are few places which are tricky to get into. What was also of note was that a very few of its occupants have a keen eye or are vocal on what they see. Perhaps the most attentive of its inhabitants are the captives and the cleaning staff but the uniformed and more elite personnel, namely the admin and higher ranking officers, couldn't give a damn as to what goes on around them. A cleaner would be able to tell any visitor looking for a detective where that detective was or when they left and what that detective was dressed in, whereas the officer at the front desk would not even be able to describe what the detective looks like physically. The front desk officer cannot even say what the detectives' office number is but the cleaner can enlighten on not only the office number but the telephone extension as well. The prisoners on the other hand can tell who of the on shift officers is reasonably watchful or who is more civilised and even most shady. The crooked cops are the ones that they mostly prefer because they are the ones that would be able to smuggle in contraband for them or help them jump bail, either by opening the gate and letting them walk free or by connecting them to the detective who can alter the charge sheet or make the entire dossier disappear. This, I found out on one of the nights that I took up accommodation in their spacious suites, for the second time. I am not sure which was more peculiar about this situation; the fact that I was not arrested or charged, malicious or otherwise, for any criminal misconduct like the last time or that I actually went back into a cell.

Nonetheless, it was more of the police's bid to do community services because I knew that I couldn't rightly walk up to the officer in charge and ask to check out their cells; that would have taken me forever and I would probably still be waiting for the approval from Pretoria, if I would ever get one. So the next best thing was for me to let myself in and from watching the cars I noted that from time to time the SAPS will offload members of the faceless society and put them up for the night. This was also evident in the fact that on some mornings, just after shift change, a dishevelled figure would appear at the vehicle entrance and waiting for the right moment, I approached them and enquired from them what they were arrested for. Most would take the time to talk to me and tell me that were picked up at a place where they were suspect to cause a disturbance or there is a high crime rate, like outside a shopping centre or a jewellery stores. They were never processed, just placed into an unlocked cell and left there for the night. In the morning they would get the English breakfast and then be on their merry way. In order for me to take advantage of the situation, all I had to do was to dress in some old clothes and blanket that I had urinated in, soiled with sorghum beer and buried them for a week and when I unearthed them I almost brought up the contents of my stomach and I knew that there would be no way that any member of the SAPS would want to manhandle me or come too close to me to get a proper identification for that matter.

Throughout the entire time of my investigations, I forced myself to do something that I had told myself that I would never do in my marriage: I twisted the facts about to Nthabi regarding my whereabouts and my activities. I put it across to her that I was on the road to recovery from the trauma of having being locked up and that I was doing some late night community service like working in a soup kitchen. I had always told her how therapeutic cooking was for me and through that I had been able to work through some of my problems. She was not too convinced about the whole matter but she was also accepting of the fact that I had an altruistic side that I did not suppress. In as much as I had told her on previous occasions that I was not really a fan of the human race, I still believed that there were some people that deserved help and attention. I would tell her at times that I had gone off to Hammanskraal and would be back in the early hours of the morning or just before I had to take her to work. I really didn't like what I was doing with regards to the truth but I had to do what I was doing and at the same time I had to protect her and the kids from harms way. The way I figured it was that should my prey get another opportunity to turn predator, they would ensure that this time they really clean house and if there was any way that they could link my current activities to my family then they would definitely take full advantage of that. If it should happen that the bogey-police return they could arrest everyone but a savvy prosecutor and magistrate would see that only I was the victim of the arrest, so the best way I could protect them at this point was to leave them completely out of the picture. I have been lied to before and I know what it truly feels like, it hurts; it hurts like nothing that I can compare to in the physically realm. It's not a pain that I would want to inflict upon anyone that I know, care for or love and in anyway that I diced this matter it was wrong for me to lie to her and the kids. I would find myself, for the first time since this whole saga began, thinking intently about what I stood to lose. I would ask myself during the stake-outs if all I was doing was really worth the emotional trouble that it could bring with it and still I could not justify the lies. They certainly were necessary but not justifiable not by any account. I sometimes contemplated telling her truth but would sooner ask myself, before I had even finished the thought, what would she then do after she knew the truth; worry? Join me on this crusade because she's the type of woman who would do just that? It's not that I would mind her company but she was now the bread winner and where would she get the energy to do all these extra curricula activities? The one way I knew that these lies were going to be perceived was that I was having an affair and even that was just ghastly. There truly was no better of the two evils. I could only pray that when the whole sordid matter was over she would understand and that the surveillance records that I had been keeping would vindicate me. I could not afford to lose her yet there I was going ahead and doing almost everything that could play a major part in achieving that.

On one hot summer's afternoon after dropping Nthabi off at work for one of her nightstop flights, I headed out to go retrieve my dinner suit from its hiding place. However, I must say that there is something grossly suspicious about a man holding a shovel in the veld and walking about tracing his footsteps, a child would probably take it that he's playing pirates and looking for buried treasure but to an adult the first thing that comes to mind is whose body is he digging a hole for. Dubious behaviour or not, I had to retrieve my evening wear as I had unscheduled reservation at the local Chez Prefecture and though I was becoming a ball of nerves, my anger was still leading the way and I was not going to mess with my date. With every stroke I took with that shovel, I felt that anger that had been stored welling up, concealing and finally consuming the nervousness. When I finally reached the object of my dig, I was sweaty and completely enraged which was just the type and amount of energy I needed for the day. I didn't need compassion or guilt or any of that soft stuff, I had to be fuelled by unadulterated fury which I could turn to grit in order to carry on with this insanity. There was no space for remorse because I was sure that wherever they were, my conspirators did not have any of that in their vaults of emotions. The parfum du stench of the clothes was just barely masked by the smell of the refuse I had taken from the house. It was approximately 18h00 when I parked the car at the airport staff parking and found a camera shy, urine smelling spot to change clothes and put on an overall to further disguise and in a plastic bag I carried my blanket and the rest of my disguise. I slipped out of the parking lot using a relatively unknown exit. The town centre where I was sure to find police activity at night was within 4km and I knew that the sweat I would work up from that walk would add a more believable element.

Along the way, I blemished my face with shoe polish with a slight mix of dirt just so that I could really appear unbathed. I worked the remnants of the polish that was on my hands deep into them so that they would seem scarred and reptilian. I shoved some snuff up my nostrils to get me to sneeze so that I could get a runny nose effect going; nobody likes a snot nosed bugger in their company. Whatever excess mucus I had I kept wiping off onto my sleeves and lapels. I was sure that not even my mother would recognise me in the state I was in and having shed the overall and taken a few swigs of sorghum beer mixed with cheap whiskey and swirled it in my mouth a couple of times, I appeared staggering and unashamed from my en route change room: behind the bushes with my blanket and plastic bag with the beer and whiskey concoction inside ready as I could ever be for the public. A few blocks from the taxi rank, I spotted an ex-colleague from the airport and in effort to test the facade, I headed towards him. I had an axe to grind with him because I had seen him abuse his check-in code and on several occasions I had heard him brag about how he would solicit and accept money from customers so that he would waiver their excess baggage charge. What would happen is that a passenger would come to the counter with more than 20kg of baggage and instead of directing the passenger to the ticket and sales counter so that they can pay for extra weight per kilo, he would suggest that the passenger do something for him like buy him a cold drink; which actually meant pay him a far less than what the company would ask for the excess. He would then falsely record the passengers' baggage as being within the permissible weight and as he was tagging the bags with the automated baggage tags, he would accept his payment from his customer and only then give them their boarding pass. He was an extortionist and a well practised one at that and what was getting to me was that he was not only getting away with it but he was also teaching the younger and newer agents how to ply his trade. By doing this he was ensuring that whenever he was called in for questioning because some guppy got caught out and they fingered him, he would have plausible deniability. After all how feasible was it that he was the sole mastermind behind such a widespread practise?

He had been standing on the sidewalk scratching about in his backpack and when I got closer to him, I coughed something heavy to make sure that he would take note of my approaching presence; he gave me one glance and continued with what he was doing, so I took a swig of my brew and started hurling insults like the mad drunk that I wanted to be seen as. With each swaggering disjointed and staggering step that I took closer to him, the contents of my plastic bag rattled harder and harder as they knocked about inside. The coughing and insults did not seem to phase him much so I embarked on a more obtrusive tact as I began to gibber and lean towards him and that caught his attention, irritatingly, he looked up and I made sure that I breathed on him as heavily as I could and sure enough he reacted just the way I had imagined he would. He immediately jolted back, clutched his backpack and covered his nose, two seconds later he was puckering his lips and trying as hard as possible not to retch. Being the more sober of the two, he quickly crossed the road disappeared into the thinning evening crowd. I wanted to jump up and down from the success of the exercise and shout out

'Ja! You only got just a bit of what you rightly deserve you cretinous bugger!'

That act was just what I needed to boost my confidence so I continued on my adventure and sought some bleeding heart or unsuspecting night shift cops that would pick me up and help me with my plan. Their patrols were more likely to run in the bank concentrated area, the vicinity of the jewellery stores and definitely, most definitely by the night shift scarlet women. Having been on several nights out on the town, I had seen that cops usually patrol heavily where there are hookers and where they get an opportunity, they will cop a feel in exchange for the girl's freedom, almost like the girls paying their toll fees for walking the streets on their beat. I was not feeling too competitive, so I was going to avoid the hooker district and it also just didn't seem too appealing to have some horny cop trying to feel me up which meant that I had to go to banking district. All I had to do there was to just put my blanket on the ground, assume a sleeping position and wait for my lift. The public are scared of vagrants, especially if they are close to automated teller machines or places made to be of convenience for them; it will take a bit of time but someone will call the police and they will come to investigate. The first to arrive on the scene was a rent-a-cop guy who was just armed with a baton, a torch and a two-way radio. If I could get him agitated enough, he would eventually radio his colleague who would then call for back-up. The back up would come either in the form of their patrol car or a police van. If one of their patrol cars pulled along then I would have to continue with the agitation until a police van was called in. As a dirty, stinking drunk it was not very difficult to agitate the rent-a-cops; they would come over to my sleeping spot and get close enough to get my eau de natural and then take a step back and start prodding at me to check that I was alive. Once they had established that I was living, they then insultingly command me to move along. Being in a drunken state, I made sure that it took me a long time to even attempt standing up. The more I slipped and slid all over the sidewalk, the more they were getting worked up because the way I stank up the neighbourhood, they could not even touch me to help up. I was relishing in the moment because they wanted me gone but they would not even touch me. They were getting weary of my antics and one of them finally suggested that they call the police to come take me away and lock me up for the night and for me that statement was like music to my ears and it rooted me on and I jabbered ever so convincingly, spitting and farting at any given chance. I was being a downright menace to them. When they couldn't take the abuse any further they opted to leave me there on the sidewalk to wait for the police. It was almost four hours later when the police van came by to check out what all the hoo-ha was all about and by then my muscles were aching from being on that hard concrete but then I was also exercising them for what lay ahead in the cells.

In their usual self-important and machismo manner, the police approached the scene and started asking some really daft questions. Before even getting close to me, they were already telling off the rent-a-cop, berating him something vicious. I really felt pity for the man but I was doing that which had to be done. It took the police a further hour to decide if they were going to shoo me off the scene or take me to the station and what an entertaining hour it was. It started off with the questioning of the rent-a-cop which led to his patrol car returning to the scene to justify to the cops why I was a nuisance and then a major argument broke out regarding whether it was really the police's function to remove vagrants from the streets or not. At this point I wanted to sit up because my body was really taking a knock from the cold concrete and watch them as they went at each other. The whole thing really broke down when the rent-a-cops emphatically told the cops what they had to do. No one, absolutely NO ONE tells a police officer what to do, especially when they are in uniform.

Everything the police do when they are in uniform is an official duty from toilet duty to picking up dry cleaning to picking up wives, girlfriends, prostitute girlfriends and their pimps, kids, brothers, sisters, cousins, uncles, parents, grand parents, great grand parents and especially when they are doing the grocery; it has all been official duty and it has always been the citizen who pays them for these laborious tasks and not what they were enlisted for. One might think that these statements are wild accusation but the police themselves confirm them through their daily actions. I have often heard police officers demand to be served first at various locales because they were on duty and that in itself has led me to believe that their career was to thwart out these damn niggling chores and that the actual task of combating crime was the duty delegated to the citizens themselves. Every so often some liaison officer would come out in the media and appeal to the public to assist the local PD by coming forward with information regarding criminal activity or information that would lead to the arrest of suspects and they also place emphasis on the public to be especially vigilant in reporting crime, however when it gets down to the actual performance of the task, very little is done. This was further evident when going through some neighbourhoods where there would be indication of criminal intent or activity taking place, in full view of the police patrols and nothing would be done to diffuse the scene or to apprehend the suspects; if anything, a siren would blare to raise the people's attention and once they had drawn their attention to the noisy wailing, the police would indicate to the people to move out of the way because they were on their way to execute their official duties. Any attempt to flag the patrol down to alert them of the crime would result in the notifier being held or even detained for obstructing them when they were carrying out of their tasks and all because they were being told what to do.

A couple of somnolent grunts and shuffles seemed to shift the attention away from the heated argument and reminded all the parties as to why they were gathered there on that sidewalk in the banking district of town, that late in the evening. Looking back, I should have rather let the bickering go on for a while longer until they resolved their issues because as soon as the yelling and threatening lulled and the police approached me and I was sworn at with every conceivable body part of my mother, from her head right down to her toes. All that profanity did not change the fact that they had to come closer to me or even pick me up to hurl me into the back of their van and that seemed to irk them even more

'Masipa a mmaye! E ye thutetsi, nat nja e!' (His mother crap, this dog's pissed himself wet) revolted the one older cop as he got to me.

I took exception to that as I only smelled of urine and wanted to correct him on his false perception but it was the hard unexpected boot straight to the anus which knocked the wind out of me and kept me quiet. It felt as if that cop's boot was deeply wedged in my lower abdomen and busy clearing out any excrement that was in there. From that excrutiating blow, I was thoroughly convinced that that cop had been trained in the art of plugging holes with his foot and I also knew for a fleeting moment how it felt like to be a rugby ball and to receive the full might of a kicker. I was still reeling in shock and pain when a follow up was made with a well placed boot stomping on my thigh, numbing it of whatever little feeling was left there. In as much as I wanted to yelp out like a mangy mutt, I soon realised that any cries of pain would initially shock my torturer and then spurn him on to inflict even more pain as he would have to cover up his folly. I cringed and winced as the blows rained in and muffled and stifled each cry that wanted to be heard, however the pain increased and I was just about to explode when it all stopped just as it had begun.

My biggest fear was not that of ending up in hospital or on a cold slab in the morgue but rather the fact that they could break me and the hidden surveillance equipment, especially the camera that I had on me.

'E constable, a re nke masipa a, re lo oa koalla pele re oa bolea!' (Constable, let's go lock this piece of shit up before we end up killing it). I wanted to say 'Good call, I fully support that suggestion and would you fellas mind if we started at the drug store for some pain killers, I have a strong sobering headache here?'

'Hey, uena security ea masipha! Ho na le ho o boneng mo? Ye! Jou, moeskont! Voetsak, tsamo kata tjelete ea magoa, mididi. Nxa!' (Hey, shitty rent-a-cop! Did you see anything here? Did you? You vermin! Bugger off and go guard the white man's money you pauper.) The Sergeant exclaimed as they backed off me.

Somehow during the pummelling they had become immune to the stench and they picked me up and flung me into the back of their van and we were on our way to the station. We must have taken the scenic route to the station because what ordinarily would have been two minute drive from where I was picked up, took almost thirty minutes and supposedly through the hills and valleys of the city and they seemingly found every pothole in the city and drove through it. Through the humming of the van and the Thobela FM broadcast, I could make out the police radio squawk where there were calls coming in from as far as Pretoria. The calls were about car and truck jackings, house break-ins, domestic violence, neighbours complaining about the noise from their neighbours, gun shots being fired, follow ups on calls that were made earlier and that's where I featured.

'Er! Ja Kilo Papa one to control. We find suspect. It's just old drunk but, er no threat. We gonna take him to homeless place but no response there so we bring him to station just now! Over!'

'You cretinous vermin, who are you calling old?' I murmured as we drove through another pothole and the impact of my body bashing against the bakkie floor lent its own weight to the previous beating.

'Kilo papa one, confirm; you are bringing the suspect to the station. Over!' the radio controller crackled over the waves.

'Ja man, e taue ntho e; ha tsebe le ho bua! Over!' (Yes man, this thing is so drunk it can't even talk! Over!), the sergeant boomed back to the control room. 'O batla ke etseng ka eona, ke see mo strateng? Ye? Bua man! Over!' (What do you want me to do leave it here on the street? Speak man! Over!), he continued as he sped over a speed hump.

'Yooo!' I slurred out from my cabin in the back just as a courtesy reminder that he actually has a living human being in transit.

'Otloa fela, masipa ke hona a otloang bohloko. Ha ro lahlela ntja e ko li seleng, o tla folla moo, ba ba ho seng ba tla bona hore batsoa joang ka eena.' (Just listen, the shit only just felt pain. Let's go dump this dog in the cells, he'll recover there and the morning shift we'll see to finish with him.), he declared to his constable.

Thank goodness for small, smelly mercies because I could not take the joyride any further, my stomach was so topsy-turvy I could have thrown up at any moment.

'Daai goed donder eng seele ke lakatsa kuku man, ha ree ro mo sea re be feta rethola bo makgosha ba babeli ree thuse ka bona ho ntsa stress! (That beating has left me quite horny, let's go dump him and then go find two hookers to unwind with), the sergeant coo-ed as we drove into the rear of the police station.

Before they opened their doors and I could hear footsteps approaching and a voice similar to the one I heard earlier from the other side of the radio conversation began rasping at the sergeant but before he even concluded his deluge, he was met with the stench which was seeping through the back windows. It would seem that he and the driver of the car were on the same rank because the constable kept responding using sergeant and no higher rank. The constable was ordered to get me out of the back and prop me up against the van so the radio sergeant could have a look at me. I wasn't too bothered about being identified because the van was parked facing the big halogen courtyard lamp, so we were pretty much in the shadows of the bakkie itself. Thanks to the dead leg they had given me at the pick up, I was able to convincingly jelly and wobble while I slurred my speech to the greatest possible extent. The radio sergeant took one look at me and shot back two steps while the patrol sergeant came closer to help his constable, with my head slightly bobbing, I took aim and waited for the right moment for him to speak because by then I knew that he was such a vociferous and vulgar person and he would say something about my mother's body parts again but I was going to make sure that that would be the last thing he said about mom. As soon as he opened his pie hole, I launched the contents of my stomach out at him like guided missile making sure that as much as possible exploded on his face and the bulk of it finding its way into his mouth and down his throat. The constable shrieked as dropped me like hot potato, while his sergeant sourly swallowed and gagged from the virulent vomit and almost tripped up on the radio sergeant behind him. The radio sergeant who was still disgusted by the smell pushed him back towards me where he landed squarely face first onto the once urine drenched jacket. That blow to my chest just urged me to fart as loudly as possible and the sorghum beer was abundant in that relief. Once the radio sergeant had taken another two steps back and regained his balance he bellowed in laughter and if it was not for the van that pulled in just as the patrol sergeant had pulled me to my feet, he would have unleashed a deadly blow straight into my face. The officer who came out reprimanded him and it would seem that he knew that it was a higher ranking officer so he too dropped me like a hot potato and stood to attention. With vomit oozing down his face, spit dripping on his chin and his nostrils flaring like those of a thoroughbred, he stood chest out and stomach in to the commands of the inspector. When the inspector heard their version of whole incident, which was laced with untruths, he battled to contain the laughter, especially when they got to the part of me regurgitating, as he ordered the constables to take me to the cells. The hot potato was once again picked up and helped to the cells, where he would be given accommodation as was intended from the onset.

As we made our way to the cells, I could hear the roar of laughter from other night shift cops who came to investigate what the stir was all about and amongst it, were some sniggers of pity and the fainting vulgarity and gagging from the patrol sergeant. I once again began with my senseless ramblings, spruced with utterance of boroko (sleep) and my disgusted guides just kept on agreeing with my notion of sleep and reassured me that I would be going to get some sleep shortly. When we entered the main cells' courtyard they howled at the officer in charge asking for a cell and one whiff from the pungent odour and he made a bee-line towards a cell and for the two accompanists, the old geezer seemed to take forever to open the huge iron gate. My heart raced faster as the key turned and the gate clanged; my thoughts bounced between 05 March 2010, the last time I was in those cells and all the other times I have had to go into a jail cell and I nearly burst out pleading mercy that all this was a bad joke but there was no turning back at that point. If I had even showed them an inkling of sanity or sobriety, it would have meant a world of pain and probable disappearance from the face of the earth. He finally opened the first gate and started on the second one leading into the individual cell's inner court-yard, where the prisoner get some sunshine and stretch their legs. He took a couple more steps leading towards the cell itself and worked on that lock, all the time we were waiting in the first gate for him to give the clearance to enter so that I could be dumped and this was more of a precautionary measure because the two constables had not checked in their guns at the processing office, so there was a risk that they could be pounced and disarmed by an inmate. The jail keeper flipped on the light, peered into the cell and then opened the last gate, he was content that it was safe for us to enter and he beckoned to us. I was dragged in and dumped on the floor just by the door, all the time with their own commentary and profanity.

The patrol constable's bravado and arrogance, along with all its vulgarity had waned considerably and his disbelief and humanity began to surface as the three officers stood at the cell door looking at me and listening to me babble softly in a lulling manner. Once the gate keeper was satisfied that all was well, he enquired about what had happened and the patrol constable related the story as he lit a cigarette. The old man chuckled as he bummed a smoke from his young colleague and they stood there for some time smoking and their attention veered more to the old timer who then shared some of his experiences involving vagrants. He assured the young cops that this was a common occurrence and that the following morning, usually before the arrival of the top brass or after breakfast, the vagrants were let out and some would leave before then by shift change and for that reason they, the cell officers, wouldn't lock these cells but they do tell the oncoming shift of any vagrants in a cell, which was usually that particular one that I was in. The conversation then shifted towards other inmates and how dangerous they were or how connected they were. He started telling them about one of the prisoners who was arrested for assault and how this guy was willing to make it worth any officer's while if that officer was willing and able to swing the case and make it a lesser charge like common assault or even bungle up the charge sheet. Before the old man could conclude his story, the patrol inspector, entered into the cell and the cell guard called for attention, the inspector made some feeble attempt at being upset at the gathering and enquired about the vagrant that had spewed on one of his officers. He dismissed the two constables, who were then standing at attention and because of his unexpected entry, were unable to properly discard their cigarettes. He took the smoke from the constable's hand and made a fuss about the rules and regulations regarding smoking in State owned premises and violently stomped it out. The constables scurried out and their footsteps could be heard trailing towards the main courtyard and once he heard the reverberation of the main gate, he continued to address the old man, who was now standing at ease. He stepped into the cell and prodded me with his boot to check if I was conscious, I graciously responded with a groan and some stored up flatulence and he backed off.

'Hy's poep dronk, ne?' (He's utterly drunk, isn't he?), he asked still with his head still in the cell.

'Daai een is heeltemal uit' (That one's completely out), responded the guard, who seemed more relaxed.

'Nou, wat's die storie wat jy se vir die jongspan?' (Now, what's this story that you're telling these youngmen?) he said as he reached into his pocket and pulled out his pack of smokes.

'Ek vertel hulle net van party gevangenise wat ons hier kry' (I was just telling them about some prisoners that we get here).

'Ja ne, Mokone. You and your jailhouse stories,'

'Our boy's getting really jumpy in there. How are things going on your side?' Sergeant Mokone commented and I lay still, thinking that if they were referring to me but it was quite improbable as I hadn't moved that much since I got prodded a minute or two ago.

'Daai laaitie is in diep kak' (That boy is in deep shit), the Inspector responded with some concern in his voice and this just added more confusion because earlier on I was being referred to as an old drunk now I was being called a 'laaitie'.

'So waar! Maar ea spaneha sak ea hae?' (That's true! But is his case workable?), Mabitla quizzed as he took a drag from his cigarette.

'Hy's vokken dapper maar dom. Hoe het hy geweet om jou te vra' (He's fucken brave but stupid. How did he know to ask you?)

'Een van sy bende, miskien. Hy wou nie se nie!' (One of his gang, perhaps. He won't say!)

'Watte een? Het hy nog nie gese nie?' (Which one? Has he not said yet?)

'Nog nie! Het jy sy leer gekry?' (Not yet! Did you get his file?)

'In my sak.' (In my bag), the Inspector responded with a certain amount of cockiness.

'Mokone; o se tlaela, oa tseba! O se tlaela sa nnete. Genuine! O sure ho re bo mme ba rona ke bana ba motho? Why would you leave it in your bag?' (Mokone; you're an idiot, you know! A real idiot! Genuine! Are you sure our mothers are sisters?) Mabitla's voice became gruff and agitated as he fanned his hand in front of his eyes signalling to his cousin how stupid his actions were.

'Hey! Kgetha matsoe a hau! Jou vokken poephol!' (Hey, choose your words! You fucking asshole!)

'Monna (Man), all I'm saying is that what if this guy's trying to set us up?'

'Listen Sergeant! This is not going to be any different to any other shakedown that we've done before. I'll go get the file and you can see for yourself.'

'So are you going to bring the file or are we just going to spend the night idly chatting?' the Sergeant asked.

'Shit man, keep your pants on; I'll go get it! So who's been here to visit him?'

'The usual; a worried ou tannie (aunty), a bunju (a young girl) who's probably some slut he's pomping and one or two lokshin vuilpops (township boys)'.

They dragged the final pulls of their cigarettes, puffed the smoke up into the air and headed out. Mabitla asked about and offered to close and lock the cell for his cousin, my heart pounded at hearing those words but Mabitla reassured him that there was no need and that they would be returning to chat with their prospective benefactor in there anyway. The fading conversation crossed between the maternal insulting and the prospect of making a tax free mid-month salary. I lay there not believing what luck had befallen me, I had started on this escapade to get some information about what goes on in the cells and with the anticipation that I would have to go back more than once to get a scoop as big as what I had received that night. I was eager to find out more but could not risk being found out, so I took a few minutes to gather up my thoughts and check that my recording equipment was still in order. Once I was satisfied that all was still working, I followed the lingering cigarette smell from the two enterprising cousins. I quietly staggered and dragged my feet as if I had just woken up from a deep drunk sleep and headed towards the main gate and upon hearing the footsteps approaching from the free world, I slurred and leaned up against the gate stalling the entrance of the oncoming traffic. From the disgust in his voice, I made out that fortunately it was Mabitla and he called out to either one of the guards to come let him in. Mokone responded to the call only to find a drunk, seated vagabond blocking the gate. He sneered as he clasped my ankles and pulled me a few metres away from the gate to let his cousin in. The smell revolted Mabitla so much that he just handed Mokone a paper and told him that he would return soon, he had to take care of his constable. Mokone told his cousin to bring something to drink when he returned, probably as a peace offering for the earlier altercation and with that Mabitla left and Mokone was left with the task of getting me back to my suite.

He reluctantly stood me up and shuffled me back to the cell and when we got to the door, I just plopped myself on top of him and in his attempt to keep me off, he shoved the paper between us and that managed to give them a good smearing of vomit and I knew that that would render them useless to him. He pushed me back using the paper and it stuck onto my chest, he swore at me something solid, probably the best in his vulgar lexicon, as he hovered above me trying to retrieve his valuable document. After a few minutes of him trying to get to my chest and me wriggling about on the ground with every attempt he made to put his hand on me, I clutched my chest and mumbled out some derivative of Nthabi's name.

'Hey voetsak uena, ha ke cheri ea hao! Mphe pampiri eo, jou moeskont!' (Fuck off; I'm not your girlfriend! Give me that paper, you bugger!), he rapped as he made another attempt, his arms reaching for my body and retracting almost instantaneously like a venomous snake striking at it's prey.

'En nou, wat maak jy met jou cheri daar?' (And now, what

are you doing with your girlfriend there?'), asked an alarmed Mabitla from behind.

'Hei man! Masipa a a tsoeri daai papier!' (Hey man, this piece of shit has got that piece of paper!)

'How did this happen? Never mind! That paper so full of piss and vomit that we wouldn't be able to read it anyway. I'll go make another printout, you get the dealer in the mean time!' he mused as he handed Mokone a half-jack of whiskey.

Mokone left and returned moments later with a cuffed prisoner, whom he led into the cell and started chatting to him in a friendly manner as he freed him from the shackles. Most of their chit chat was centred on his stay in Mokone's abode and if he had been mistreated by any of the other police or prisoners. He offered him a smoke and something to drink and they continued to make idle conversation and he eased into the reason why they were sitting in a relatively empty cell. The prisoner not wanting to find himself with further complications in his life, answered very cautiously and at first showed some hesitance to be drawn into the bribery matter. He kept on asking about the smelly bundle in the cell courtyard and Mokone re-assured him that there was no threat there but he didn't buy into that story that easily so Mokone suggested that he could go see for himself. He cautiously got up and started towards me and then stopped when he realised that the door was wide open.

'Haa, what kind Vader?' (What kind of set up is this officer?)

'Huh?' Mokone responded in shock.

'Mangi fika ku leya dedlana uzo ngibakgaza bese bathi bengi funa uku baleka!' (As soon as I get to that door, you'll shoot me and it would seem as I was attempting to escape!)

'Lalela la s'boshwa! Uwe ube u ncengana nami kuthi ngikucede manje uzo ngitshela amasimba!' (Listen here prisoner! You were the one pleading with me to help you; now you stand there telling me shit?)

'Ngiya sazi i'skim sami, bak' kgafile kuthi ungcishe!' (I know how my outfit operates, they paid you to silence me!), the fear in his voice was beginning to pour out.

'Now listen here, you piece of shit. If you carry on like this; I'll let you sit here and wait out your bail and then you'll get transferred to the big house and rot there waiting for your trial.' Mabitla, said clearly irritated as he headed towards him with the cuffs in his hands again.

'Hai ne sori vader, ase ringe. Ubani lo lele laphansi e baleni?' (Sorry sir, let's talk. Who is that lying there on the floor in the courtyard?)

'That piece of shit lying there in the courtyard is some drunk one of our patrols picked up earlier tonight. Why don't you go see for yourself?'

First it was a gentle nudge with his foot that stirred me and when he was convinced with that, I got a rapid succession of kicks to the butt and lower back. The barrage was stopped by a loud crack, the familiar sound of flesh upon flesh, especially open palm on the face. Inspector Mabitla was in the house and it was the second time that this man had come to my rescue in the same night and I was beginning to like him for that, he had such impeccable timing.

'Hey uena, jy dink die is jou eie kickboxing gym?' (Hey you, you think that this private kickboxing gym?) Mabitla demanded

'What the f...?' he never even had a chance to finish that statement and another slap shut his mouth for him.

'Watch you language!' ordered Mabitla.

'Sorry Vader...!' whimpered the inmate as he backed off towards the closest wall.

'Ey rubbish, you said you want help what's your story?' quizzed Mabitla as he bent over to pick up the re-print he had dropped during the disciplinary session of the inmate.

This guy was pretty shaken up after his informal introduction to Mabitla that he forgot all about the presumed sting and assassination; he was talking to one cop which he could identify and another which he could not even make out because they were standing in the moonlit courtyard. He calmed down and stated to the two cops that he was willing to pay them handsomely if they could help him lessen the charge or break free from captivity. He assured them that he was genuine and good for the money; all it would take was one call from him to his crew and they would bring the payment, wherever he chose to meet them but he needed guarantee that they would meet their end of the bargain. Mabitla rattled off the guys name and some background details, along with some prior arrests. This guy was a definite habitual criminal and an accomplished one at that. The call sign 'Vader' should have tipped me off; it's a colloquial term that inmates use to call warders in prison or police officers. It gave the warders a higher sense of being and authority because amongst the warders and officials, rank exist but as far as the inmates are concerned, they then become rank-less but still superior beings. He sweetened the deal further by saying that he would make sure that they got a monthly allowance for whatever information that they could bring to him to help him stay out of jail and a step ahead of his competition. The way this guy was talking, it certainly sounded as if he had the money and was willing to part with it in wheelbarrows just to get out of there. He realised that he had them hooked and not even one cent had been discussed and these cops were now eating out of the palm of his hands and he was relishing in it, it was also quiet evident from his roll that he had been in this type of negotiation before. He knew what to say to them and when to say it; he was a real salesman and a charmer of note. From time to time he would ask to make that one call that would get the money closer to the cops. With only his desperation to guard against, he daringly put it to the duo to state their price.

'R25 000!' grunted Mabitla and before he could get an answer,

'A PIECE!' Mokone added, clearing his throat.

'Hai bo-Vader, you're killing me...'

'Listen you piece of cowpat from the way you were going on a second ago, it clearly shows that you have that type of money and you are not some low lying foot soldier in your organisation. You should be glad we're giving you the discounted deal,' chuckled Mabitla.

'Now for the monthly gift, we expect no less a steady 10k each' chirped Mokone.

'We'll get the information to you as and when we feel or when we get the appropriate information. Deal?!?' Mabitla said as he extended his arm to seal off the negotiations with a handshake.

'Snyman, when we walk out of here, the deal is off and its off to the big show for you and this time it will be without any possibility of parole and you can be sure that one of your compadres will take out a hit on you and we wont even have to worry about you fingering us on this conversation. EVER! So do we have a deal or not?'

'Ah Vader! Now that you put it like that I definitely see the bigger picture. We have a deal!!'

'Warra, tolla mfan' ona phone ea hae, ke sa losheba lipampirir tsa hae hore li eme joang.' (My brother, get this boy his phone, I'm going to check the status of his paperwork.)

'Tsoara, here's a pack of smokes, sit chill and relax whilst I get you your phone. Where's your prisoner's item receipt. I need to see where your shit has been stored.'

Mokone took the number from the receipt and headed to his

processing office whilst his cousin went to do his bit in the main cop shop.

'Ey moegoe! Jy los die dronkie uit. Verstaan?' (Hey twit! You leave that drunkard alone. Understand?) Mabitla barked his departing orders to Snyman.

'Dankie Vader. Sho Vader.' Snyman acknowledged both cops as they exited and he squatted a few metres away from me where he had been pinned against the wall.

CRIMINAL INTER ALIA

Contrary to many an urban myth, black people are not born as criminals just as white people are not born with silver spoons.

In the township 'Snyman' was the colloquial name or nickname given to any drug peddler but this guy was the real deal, a real pusher. Fezile Shinga was his name and he was first arrested for possession of weed at the age of fifteen years. He did nine months in stout school and upon his release the distance between him and the classroom grew bigger and bigger. He ventured further into crime, first through house breaking, which saw him being accommodated in juvie hall for a year, where he met up and befriended a young inductee of the 3SG (3 Star Gang). He just kept the hoodlums' company but never really joined the gang then until later when he got released and even then he became their consultant and in return they protected him. Each day his relationship with his family, which was then his parents and two younger siblings; a brother and a sister, became more and more strained. His father was a long distance truck driver and his mother was one of the tea ladies at some big corporation in Tshwane. Being the dedicated and passionate truck driver he was his father was on the road more than he was at home and quite often, the timing of everything was just out of sync. Firstly, his work schedule was erratic because of the mechanical breakdowns and loading or delivery delays or the overtime he had to put in which made it near impossible for him to see his family all at once. Secondly; because his wife and kids would be at work and at school by the time he was fresh and revived, there was no one in the house to talk to, so he would go out and shoot the breeze with his neighbourhood friends. However, it was just the one incident that turned his ever loving and devoted son away from him.

When Fezile was about to turn sixteen, he went back home during the long break to fetch some schoolwork and a book he had forgotten. Accompanied by one of his best friend and class-mates, Sandile, he rushed as this was an opportunity to see his father, even if it would have been for a few minutes and he kept on telling his buddy about how cool his father was, something that Sandile was quite aware of. They remarked on how they would be met with the cantabile jazz notes when they got through the gate and that his father would just be chilling to jazz legends and then exchanged names as if they themselves were aficionados. Sure enough when they got in the yard they heard the stereo gently pulsating out a velvety saxophone solo whilst the husky drums and clipping piano gently filled in and cloaked the energized audience. When they were just about to pass the window, he heard a syncopated groaning which rhythmically displaced some of the saxophone notes but that was something that he had heard before in jazz and intrepidly invited Sandile to pay particular attention to them. It was his way of showing off to his friend that he was a jazz aficionado just like his father. As they entered the house the audience in the stereo were going berserk, so his call to his father got swallowed up by the cheers. A second call for his father did little good, as the audience's applause and whistles were overtaken by harder and more wilful blowing of the ensemble so he decided to go find his father and present himself and his friend to him.

He peered into the sitting room where the stereo had been blaring unattended and on the table he could see a half empty beer glass and two 750ml beer bottles on the floor; one dry and empty and the other still frosty. Next to the beer glass was his father's tea mug, also half empty. Without much thought, he went on to go check if his father and his guest had not perhaps gone out through the open front door for a smoke when the boys came through the kitchen door. The music toned down as the saxophonist took a breather and a trumpeter took over for a solo. Within that breve of the solo change over, the groan was heard again but this time more pronounced and with a thud, he turned back into the house to find Sandile standing at a bedroom door, peeping through the crack of the door by the hinges and before he could exclaim, Sandile was shushing him and beckoning him over to come see. Fezile was not too impressed with his friend's actions, so he flung him away from the door but once again his friend motioned for him to maintain stealth and to look through the door. Reluctantly Fezile propped his face against the door and there his dad was, lying naked on his back on the bed with this unidentifiable naked person kneeling astride over him, whilst his father gave him fellatio. As his father's head bobbed up and down to take in the full length of this man's member; the man groaned with ecstasy. The groans become more and more intense as his father bobbed and sucked faster and harder. As his father took the penis out of his mouth Fezile pulled away from the door, shocked and disillusioned at what he was looking at he sat flat on the floor numb. The sound of jazz was now a distant tweets and cacophony in his mind and Sandile, who was tugging at him and motioning that they should leave before the two men caught sight of them, was a slow motion blur. Sandile dragged him away from the bedroom door towards the quickest exit; the front door. Fezile was just slump and offered very little resistance as he was being dragged and Sandile tried to help him onto his feet so that they could make their getaway. When they got to the front door, under the cover of the music, Sandile whispered to Fezile that if the two men were startled or alerted to the boys' presence they would be in big trouble and that seemed to bring Fezile around. Sandile took lead of the escape and vaulted over the fence to the neighbour's house and like a new born fawn; Fezile followed barely making it over the fence. When they were about four houses down the road, Sandile, who was breathing quite heavily from all the excitement, slowed the pace down and looked to his visibly shaken friend and started to speak but stopped before he could say a word. They carried on walking until they got to the shops and he suggested that they stop for a while. They sat on the stoep and he offered to buy his friend a cold drink; Fezile, looking straight ahead at the ground, managed to nod after Sandile had offered the drink again for the third or fourth time.

Sandile returned with two 500ml cold drinks, handed one to his friend, who was still sitting there unresponsive. He cracked it open and the sound of the fizz got Fezile's attention and as he reached for the drink all he could ask was:

'Why, mara vele, ye?'

'Eish! Angazi jo!' (I don't know man)

'Yini daai ding e yenzakele? Ye?' (What just happened? Hey?)

'Angazi mfana maar wa ringa ngayo e dladleni, uzoba e jaivini!' (I don't know boy but if you talk about it at home, you'll be in trouble)

'Mina?!?' (Me?!?)

'Lalena ntwana, obviyas i ol lady a likeni vokol nga di deng. Uzo cal' uthini kuye? "Ma! Ngi bone u baba a shintsha amagera omunye ubaba lapha e khaya!" U bani vela le outie le enye?' (Listen boy, obviously your mom knows nothing about that. What are you going to start off saying to her? "Ma! I saw dad changing some man's gears here at home!" Who is that man anyway?)

'Angimbonanga e busweni' (I didn't see his face), Fezile answered softly.

'The best mfana ukuthi u dime kufika sithola kuthi u bani lela taima elinye' (The best thing is for you to keep quiet until we find out who is that other man), Sandile went on to suggest.

'Maar jo, amasimba daai ding! Amasimba!' (But man, that's just shit. Shit!), at that he began snivelling.

'Eish, hardi jo! Hardi ntwana. Kuzo lunga!' (Sorry man. Sorry boy. It's going to get better.)

At the sound of those words, Fezile buried his head in between his knees and sobbed inconsolably, repeatedly asking why. Sandile tried with all his might to comfort and calm his friend down. The other kids from school had been going in and out of the shop and the break was almost over, not knowing what else to do he suggested that they go back to school so that they wouldn't draw any trouble from the teachers. With their half drunk cold drinks, they slowly made their way back to the school.

'Sandile, mpintsh' yam. Ngiyagqula onga ringi no muntu nga di ding!' (Sandile, my friend. Please don't talk to anyone about this thing!)

'Unga wari outi yam, yimfihlakalo yethu lendaba!' (Don't worry my friend, this is our secret!)

The rest of the day was rather difficult for Fezile to go through, his mind kept on playing back the compromising position that he had seen his father in. He did not even hear the teachers or any of the lessons for the day and he missed the homework instructions. When the bell rang signalling the end of school, he just sat in his desk whilst the other kids excitedly packed away their books. Sandile came over from his desk and began packing his books for him, all the while urging him to compose himself.

'Angifuni uku buyela daar?' (I don't want to go back there)

'Waar?' (Where?)

'Edladleni!' (Home!)

'Ngiya ferstana maar uzo tchunani? Ku kini mos, weer uyazi kuthi i ol lady lako lizo hlukumezeka awungekho maka buya espanini.' (I understand but what are going to do? It's your home and you know your mom will be traumatised when she gets home from work and you're not there)

'Eish! U ma ol lady!' (My mom!)

'As' vaye; ngine cebo!' (Let's go, I've got an idea!)

'Ang' funi ukuvaya. Yini cebo lakho?' (I don't want to leave. What's your plan?)

'As lahle i-side, ngizokutshela endleleni!' (Let's go, I'll tell you along the way!)

Fezile was not too thrilled about leaving the comfort of the classroom but he knew that he could not remain there forever besides the girls were going to start cleaning the classroom.

Everyday after school there were girls rostered to carry out the chore before they went home. It was a practise in their school and numerous township schools for the girls to clean the classrooms after school; they would sweep, mop and even polish and buff the floors and they took pride in their work. Whilst the girls were cleaning the classrooms, there were boys that were also rostered to clean the grounds and they would weed the grounds, trim the grass, till the soil, water the flowers and prune the trees. Things that I only got to do voluntarily at home or as part of my detention at school. All these extra-curricular activities were done to impress upon the learners that they are part of a community and that they need to participate in the upkeep of their environment and to inculcate a sense of responsibility, accountability and cleanliness. This also instilled camaraderie and friendly competitiveness between the various groups and classes, with one bunch always wanting to better the other's efforts. It also because the learners were the ones doing the cleaning it was effective in keeping the school reasonably clean.

The two boys walked out, leaving the clamour of the girls behind in the classroom and as they walked past each classroom, each was filled with the voices of jubilant girls getting ready or already cleaning. On cheerier days he would have poked in his head into one of the other tenth grade classes to see if Sentebaleng was there. She was a pretty fellow tenth grader that he had a crush on and the way they would steal glances at each other during break, it was quite obvious that they had a liking to each other. They had bumped into each other and exchanged some greetings and pleasantries but he had not yet formally asked her out or proposed to her. When the other guys saw her they would often poke fun at him saying that he was scared to ask her out or point out that there was his girlfriend. On this particular day he just walked past her classroom and headed for the gate with Sandile.

Upon exiting the gate and when they were clear of other ears,

Sandile began telling Fezile about his plan:

'Lalela jo, siya vaya siya kini and then mina ngizozizasisa ku taima lakho den ngi tshune kuthi siya kithi siyo geleza for ama-exam!' (Listen dude, we'll go over to your place and I'll intro-duce myself to your father and tell him that we headed over to my place to study for the exams!)

'Ah jo, ngek' ispane daai plan' (No dude, that plan wont work).

'Deurakordinwat?' (Why?)

'Lesa stabani sizo funa 'kuthi si gelezele daar kimi!' (That gay will want us to study there at my place!), Fezile rattled off with-out even a second thought that he was referring to his beloved father.

'Na lapho kugrand, at least ngeke ube uloku uringa naye into ez'baya.' (Even that is fine, at least you wont be talking a lot of things with him), Sandile responded trying to placate his friend.

'Jo, angizizwa uku geleza! Ngi cwele nge fuckshit!' (Dude, I don't feel like studying. I'm really upset!)

'Manje uzo enza njani?' (Now what are you going to do?)

'Angazi jo. Niks! Ngizo dima je!' (I don't know dude. Nothing! I'm just going to keep quiet!) and with that Fezile decided to keep the whole sordid matter inside hoping that just as surreal as it was, it would fade away and become a distant memory real soon.

The two boys ambled on without anything else being said. What was usually a ten minute walk from school got stretched out as the shuffle of their feet on the road was pronounced like a microphone had been attached to the soles of their shoes, recording their footfall at each point of contact with the ground. At the last corner where they would part ways, Sandile could see how the anger and disappointment were still at prevalent on his friend. His parching lips were a gun-metal grey and his eyes withdrawn, before he could even ask if he was going to be alright; Fezile bucked forward, pushing his friend out the way and volcanoed his stomach's contents. Once. Twice. Thrice! It was so violent on the third count that he bellowed out clutching on to Sandile's shoulder digging in his thumb into the shoulder. Initially Sandile winced then he finally let out an exclamation to notify his friend that he was being subjected to immense pain but Fezile just held on as his pain intensified. He coughed and spat out the last bit of vomit, still with his hand firmly attached to Sandile's shoulder as if his arm and hand had locked. Due to the pressure from Fezile's thumb gorging itself into his joint, Sandile was now as bent over as Fezile and only when Fezile had heaved a deep breath, with his eyes red and watery, did they both manage to get upright and Sandile prised his aching and almost numb shoulder out of Fezile's iron grip.

'Fezile!? Sandile!? Ke'eng?' (Fezile!? Sandile!? What's wrong?), a shaken but sweet melodic voice enquired from behind.

It was Sentebaleng. She was accompanying Mantoa home, who lived a few streets away from Fezile when Sandile's cry of pain caught their attention. She came up to Fezile and placed her hand on his back and when Fezile looked up and saw her through his teary eyes he managed to lessen his grip on Sandile's shoulder. Sandile immediately dropped to one knee from the pain and all that could be heard from him were a string of 'Eish!'.

'Fezile! Ke'eng?' she asked again as she reached into her pocket to pull out a rolled up toilet paper.

'Tjo! Chomi, o ntsitse di kabish!' (My friend, he's spewed out cabbage!), Mantoa pointed out, as she recoiled with a look of disgust on her face.

'Fezile! O sharp?' (Fezile! Are you ok?), asked Sentebaleng as she cast a disapproving look to her friends comment and handed Fezile a bit of toilet paper to clean himself up with.

'Eish! Ngizo ba sharp,' (I'll be ok,) he stammered, 'Sandile u grand?' (Sandile are you ok?)

'Eish! Eish! Yoo! Eish! I hlombe lami jo, engathi lenqamukile' (Feels like my shoulder's dislocated), he responded in staccato, grimacing at each word as if it was just painful to even utter out the words.

'Mantoa thusa Sandile moo tu!' (Mantoa please help Sandile!), she said as she assumed control of the situation and continued to help Fezile.

With her hands still raised at chest height, Mantoa made sure that she took the long way around, tip-toeing as if she crossing over a puddle yet she was avoiding making any sort of contact with Fezile, she was visibly disgusted by the retch and making no bones about it that if she had to be in Sentebeleng's position, she would not have even come close to Fezile. Then again, she wasn't the one that had a thing for Fezile, so it didn't really matter to her.

'Mantoa! Mantoa!', yelled Sentebaleng when she saw her friend's callous canter. It was one of those yells that was accompanied with contemptuous look, the yell and look that was synonymous with an exasperated mother.

'Ah! Maar chomi li wena maar wa bona hore ho bjang fa?!' (But my friend you can see what the situation is like here?!), said Mantoa who now had a look on her face that said 'I'm doing you a favour sister, so don't be pushy'. Mantoa was just that type of girl, the ones that thought and felt that society owed them a great deal. The types that were mostly found behind the counter of tills at the retails shops and were the most apathetic and would have no second thought of 'telling a customer where to get off'.

'Mantoa, asoblif tu! Ke kopa o thuse Sandile, oa peineloa. Mo eese habo, nna ke tla tsamaesa Fezile.' (Mantoa, please! Please help Sandile, he's in pain. Take him home and I'll walk Fezile home.) Once again Sentebaleng showed her leadership but this time in a more appealing manner and that plan, though still not as grand and fitting to Mantoa's own agenda; if she ever had one, seemed to be slightly more acceptable to her.

'Eish! Nxa! Maar le wena ka bu Charlotte Magxeka ba hau!' Sandile emella re tsamaye. Emella! Ketla ho sea, tjo! Nna oska tlo ntefela. Ema re tsamaye!' (You and your Charlotte Magxeka tendencies! Sandile stand up let's go. Stand up! I'll leave you! Don't be a wimp. Stand up and let's go!)

The two sets of youths parted and just as their paths were different, so were the manners in which the ailing boys were treated. Sentebaleng kept on looking back over her shoulder as Mantoa's constant disapproval of the situation she was placed in could be heard for metres. After taking a few more steps she looked back again once she heard Sandile's irritated but pain stricken voice part-taking in the disapproval and thus began a bickering between them that could only be likened to a couple that had been married for yonks. Worried that they might just end up fighting, she and Fezile stopped but before they could even mention a word to each other about their friends, the tone of the bickering turned to bantering and they continued with their journey, alternating between banter and disapproval and pleading. Sentebaleng and Fezile just turned towards each other and Fezile managed to respond to her smile with a pain laced grin and they also continued to his house.

They were met with jazz notes as they reached the gate of Fezile's house and the front door was still open, so the notes were even more pronounced; no sooner had he set foot in the gate, his stomach failed him again and he ejected whatever remaining contents onto the lawn alongside the pathway. Sentebaleng screamed in shock as Fezile doubled over, his weight being too much for her to counter balance, they toppled to the ground. Her screams for help were muffled by the music as she manoeuvre her herself so that she could try to turn him on his side. She got a lucky break when the song stopped and her voice pierced into the house alerting whoever was inside that their help was desperately needed on the lawn. First, the movement of a curtain showed that there was somebody in the house and then a thunderous crash followed and within seconds a man bolted through the front door. He charged towards the two youths on the grass, dropped to his knees and impatiently demanded to know what was happening. A sobbing Sentebaleng tried to brief the man in as much as she could. Shaken up by he was hearing and what was happening, he vigorously patted and anxiously looked the boy up and down as if he was checking if he was armed but he was actually trying to ascertain if there were any external injuries on him. He turned Fezile onto his back and lowered his ear towards the boy's chest to listen for a heartbeat and when he managed to hear a distant but low beat he breathed a sigh of relief and told Sentebaleng to go into the house and get some water for Fezile. He picked up the young man, who had fainted and been dehydrated from vomiting and followed her into the house where he went and laid him on the couch. Sobbing and shaking, Sentebaleng returned with a jug of water and handed it over to the man who was sitting alongside Fezile and gently calling out his name trying to revive him. He placed the jug on the floor and asked her to get a glass and directed her to where she would find them in the kitchen. Whilst she was still rustling about in the kitchen getting a glass he called out to her and directed her towards where they kept some medicines and asked her to bring the packet of nausea or paracetamol tablets. She could not find the nausea and the paracetamol so she took the glass to the living room and reported that there were no nausea and paracetamol tablets. She was directed back to the kitchen to check in the cupboards alongside to see if they were possibly incorrectly placed there and if there was none then she should bring back any pain killers that she found there. Fezile was beginning to stir when she scurried back to the kitchen and in her zeal to see his recovery; she found a bottle which was labelled 'take two for pain and fever'. She grabbed the bottle and dashed back to the living room and handed it over. The man, half filled the glass with water, raised it towards Sentebaleng and asked her to pop in two tablets. He swirled the glass as he brought it back towards him and at seeing that the tablets were not dissolving quickly, he told Sentebaleng where she would find a teaspoon and to bring one back so that he could crush the tablets. He crushed the tablets but the powder still did not fully dissolve into the water, he raised Fezile's head and told him to drink. Fezile took a drink and began to sputter and cough as the water and powder made its way down his throat, he was given a bit of break and then the medicine was administered again until it was finished. More water was added to the remainder of the powder in the glass and given to him to finish off. The tablets must have been extremely bitter because he grimaced and winced and tried to raise his arm to stop the glass from getting to his mouth and shortly thereafter he feebly lowered his arm and his head went limp in the man's arms, who then laid it back on the couch and let him rest as he muttered something incoherently.

Sentebaleng's sob were reduced to sniffs as she sat opposite the two, watching what was happening. The man who was in his early fifties still seated partially on the couch turned to face her directly. He had short hair, a tired looking face with a stubble and the smell of Fezile's vomit was colliding with the smell of his deodorant which seemed like it had been applied shortly before their arrival and in between the odours was another unfamiliar, subtle and distasteful smell which seemed to pour itself into the living room from bedroom adjacent to the living room. He was tall man with broad shoulders dressed in a white vest and casual polyester pants; which sat on comfortably on his mid-sized waist and they were reminiscent of the late sixties' mapantsula dress code. He had on black socks with a diamond pattern and polished leather patterned lace up shoes, which were also quite popular during his and her father's youth.

He spoke in a slow dragging raspy voice and began to address her; she introduced herself and narrated the saga to him. She told him how she and Mantoa had come across the boys at one of the corners on their way to Mantoa's house. She did not dare to tell him that she and Fezile had affectionate feelings towards him and kept their acquaintance to being fellow tenth graders. He, in turn, introduced himself as Fezile's father and told her how eternally grateful he was that she brought his son home. He emphasised how much ubuntu she had and that it was reflective of her upbringing and good parental guidance. He offered her something to drink and she asked for water, he stood up and took the glass that he was using for Fezile and went to the kitchen. He splish-splashed it under a running tap and got some cold water from the fridge, filled up the glass and went back to her. She thankfully accepted the glass and began to drink from it without even inspecting it. When she finished, she thanked him again, excused herself and bid him farewell. Fezile's father walked her out as far as the gate and thanked her again; she was still concerned about his well being but he assured her that he'll be alright and that she was always welcome to check up on him and with that Sentebaleng headed home.

When Fezile came to, he was dressed in his pyjamas and in his bed; his head was throbbing and his stomach growling from the hunger. He was dazed and his vision was blurry but he looked around and focused on some of the familiar objects around the room. In a distance he could hear voices and one of them sounded like his mother's and he called out to her and having done that, his head pounded even harder as the room began to spin. His mother came rushing through the door to find her son trying to get out of bed but his body was not complying with his commands. She came by his bedside, helped him back into bed and shushed him. He tried again to get out and all that could come out from his mouth was:

'Amanzi...' (Water...), the word trailed off as he tried to lift his upper body and sit beside his mother.

'Ufuna amanzi?' (Do want water?), his mother asked with concern.

'Amanzi...' he repeated as he nodded.

She called out to one his siblings to bring him water and once again she lay him down on the bed. Fezile's younger brother came in with a cup of water and handed it to his mother and she rasped him to bring more in a jug. He darted out of the room almost knocking his father over, who was entering the room and when he returned looked extremely concerned and lovingly at his brother as he handed the jug over to their mother. Fezile gulped down the second cup of water and began crying as he tried to focus on his father, who was beginning to ask what had happened earlier on in the day. Fezile very much wanted to tell his mother what he had seen when he and Sandile came to the house during the school break but he just felt overwhelmed with emotion and when Sandile's words of warning about spilling the beans came back to him; he cried even harder. When his father came closer to sit down by the bed to comfort him, he cried out even harder and his head throbbed and pounded uncontrollably to the point that he could only focus on the pain.

'I-khanda!' (My head!), he shrieked out and tried moving his hands to his head in an attempt to slow down the banging,

'Fezile!' his mother called out, 'liyenze njani i-khanda?' (What's wrong with your head?), she asked in a state of panic,

'Iyoo, mama! Libuhlungu!' (It's painful!)

'Thula mtanami, ukukhala kuzo yenza khuthi lidume nokundlula' (Shush now my baby, crying will only make it pound even more)

'Zama ukuthula mfanami!', his father re-iterated but at the sound of his voice Fezile just broke down even more and curled up into a ball with his head in his hands.

Realising that the sound and sight of her husband was aggravating the situation, she asked him to leave them.

'Bab-Shinga, ngi cela usishiye si sodwa kancane!' (Mr. Shinga, could you please leave us alone for a while!). She always called her husband Baba or Bab-Shinga, it was a sign of respect and just how she was brought up; her mother called her father Baba just like her grandmother called her grandfather Baba.

Bab-Shinga reluctantly stood up and headed out of the room and his protestations echoed as he closed the door behind him. Ma-Shinga just sat next to her son and calmed him down, telling him that everything was going to be alright; she thought that her son was bawling out because he just wanted to be brave in front of his father but his body was not allowing him to do so and every time he gasped from his crying, evidently trying to speak, she silenced him and told him to relax. After some minutes Fezile calmed down and she asked him if she should bring him something to eat and that was when he recalled the grumbling stomach and nodded. She left for a while and went to prepare some soft porridge for him and whilst she was busy he could faintly hear his parents discussing the events, cross questioning each other but his father doing so more heatedly as if the whole thing were his mother's fault. She could not defend herself because she was not guilty of anything nor did she have all the facts of what happened and her main concern at that moment was her son and she just resigned herself to the ramblings on of Shinga. Fezile wished that he had enough strength to get up and face his father but the headache and hunger kept him at bay. Ma-Shinga came back into the room with umdogo (soft porridge) and she propped him up and fed him just as she used to when he was still a toddler and when he was done, just like all those years ago she said:

'Awuboni ke mfana wam!' (That's my boy!)

'Dankie ma.' (Thank you ma)

'Uzizwa unjani manje?' (How do you feel now?)

'Ngincono' (Better) he responded gently, 'Ma...Myeke uBaba' (Ma...leave dad), he said even softer,

'Ungakhatazeki ngo babakho mntanam; wena phumula konke kuzo lunga' (Don't worry about your father; rest now, everything will be alright), she said that in context of the discussion she had just had with husband whilst she was making umdogo for Fezile but he was actually telling her to divorce the man. She tucked her son in and left him to sleep.

He was woken up in the morning by the sound of his siblings getting ready for school and that obviously meant that his mother had long left for work but he asked them if she was still at home. They told him that they overheard their parents speaking and that because Bab-Shinga was still going to be at home for a couple of days to come, he would watch over him and his recovery and therefore there would not be a necessity for her to take days off from work. The thought of having to spend the days the next few days his father trouble him and it was clearly not a solution for him but what could he do. When he heard his brother telling his sister to hurry otherwise they would be late for school, he decided that would be the best thing for him to do; to go to school. His body was not in top gear but he figured that he would get by for the day, so he began to prepare himself. When his father came to check up on him, Fezile was finishing putting on his school shoes and getting ready to go spill out the wash basin that he was using. Bab-Shinga was quite astonished to see his son up and about and with that raspy dragging voice of his, he kept hounding his son with questions about how he felt and what had happened the previous day and why should he go to school. The man's voice just kept on sounding like the groans and moans that he and Sandile had heard coming from his mother's room and as each syllable came out of that mouth, images of the two men kept flashing in his head. He raised his hands to his head as it started to pound again and told his father that he had to go to school because they were writing an important term test on that day. Bab-Shinga could see that Fezile was definitely not coping with the pain and so he said that he should take the pain killers that he administered to him the previous day. Fezile wanted to have nothing to do with Bab-Shinga and out of politeness and wanting to dismiss the man's insistence; he grabbed the vial and bid him a cold and unsociable goodbye. He ran out of the yard and disappeared amongst the other pedestrians making their way to their day, there were no cheery greetings to the neighbours as he most often would on his way to school; he just wanted to be blend into the masses.

He arrived at school and avoided making conversation with any of the other kids unnecessarily, including Sandile and Sentebaleng and seeing that he had very few friends and with what he was going through, he did not want to and talk to anyone about it, it was downright embarrassing and he would be the laughing stock of the whole school. From time to time his thoughts would drift off to what he saw and he would wonder how that whole matter would have gone down if it was witnessed by one of his other friends, he was sure that they would have taken the first opportunity to notify the whole school. When the bell rang for break, Sandile flexed his shoulder and asked him how he was feeling; he jokingly mentioned that Fezile had pulled out his entire joint from its socket. Fezile wasn't sure whether to laugh as he apologised and thanked his friend. Sandile coaxed him go with him to join up with the other kids and try to put this sordid affair behind them. They got to the other boys who were hovering above some bread, chips, polony and viennas that they had all financed and every so often a hand would dip down towards them and come up with a generous handful of food. Fezile had no appetite but his head was pounding again and upon hearing that someone in the group said that whenever he got a headache he would light up a smoke and take a few puffs and shortly thereafter the headache would go away and on the backdrop of that notion another boy suggested a joint of weed and another bright spark said that a shot of brandy usually did the trick for him; whilst an even more knowledgeable teen said that a combination of all was the best because by the time the joint settled into the system the cigarette would make sure it stayed there for longer. They all swore by their methods and assured him that they worked miraculously and marvellously but further to that they teased him as being too good and clean a child to even try any of them, and in his attempt to defend himself he told them that his father had given him some pain killers and that he just wanted to have some cold-drink to wash them down. Trying to sway them away from their taunting he told them that the tablets were so potent that they knocked him out instantaneously after he took them, when they heard this the other boys roared out with laughter and said that that just proved their point that he was still a baby and the tablets were probably some over the counter paracetamol. The kid who suggested smoking a spliff said that he could probably smoke the tablet and he would still be standing after that and the brandy kid said that he could probably pop two of them and down half a bottle of brandy and still be sober after that. They continued to exchange their bravado and laughing at each others dares. Fezile pulled out the vial from his pocket and put two tablets in his hand and just as he was about to pop them in his mouth the weed kid said he would put his money where his mouth was and that Fezile should hand him a pill and they could go roll a joint and he'll prove it to all of them. Upon hearing this one of the boys suggested that they all take the rest of the day off and head for quite spot where they could really get down and relax and unhinge themselves from the stress of the tests and upcoming end of year exams. None of the boys wanted to be seen as being spineless they agreed and they all left the school yard.

Each kid popped out whatever amount they had on them and they were able to raise close to R100 and their first port of call was Mojalefa's shebeen to buy the brandy. It was the one of the many in the township that were known to sell alcohol to anyone with money, regardless of their age or colour. It was also rumoured that this was the peddle spot for any illegal recreational medication such as nyaope and the then relatively new whoonga. Further to that there were reports that Mojalefa had rooms where his elite customers could smoke up, shoot up or crank without having to worry about police raids or any other disturbances. Mojalefa's was definitely not just a spaza-cum-shebeen, it was a convenience store for social deviants, especially tweakers and the biggest and best story of that place was that Mojalefa himself was a clergyman but no-one really knew who he was. He had never been identified and the place had quite a few management changes, it were as if Mojalefa's was a vending machine, owned and maintained by a faceless corporation and it was placed in the township to generate income. Mojalefa's worked because it was not a night club which always attracted a lot of police attention, it was a house in the township, part of the neighbourhood and one of those places that had been there since the dawn of time and highly respected within the underworld. It was not a private club but it had secret or rumoured to have VIP facilities.

The boys went in and stocked up on their supplies; no questions asked, no identity required - just a straight forward cash for stash transaction and they headed for the railway line where the long grass of the veld would give them perfect cover; if the grass wouldn't work then there were the derelict buildings that would do the job. When they got to a small clearing a couple of metres from the railway line, they began unpacking their bags as if they were on a picnic. The area itself proved to be conducive because there was clear evidence all around that what they were about to engage in was a common activity that had always been taking place there. There were makeshift seats made from propped up bricks, crates, old torn seats and sundeck chairs and the ground had been slightly dug out and there were charred remains indicating that many a fire had been stoked there. Fezile wondered how the other boys knew about that place and most importantly, how did they know about what transpired there? Were they drug users? He did not have to wait long to get his answers. The one boy took three pinches of weed from its matchbox container and then began to seed it; when he was satisfied that there weren't anymore seeds in the stash, he laced it with half a crushed cigarette and the pill he took from Fezile and then he placed the mixture on some tobacco paper, which they had also purchased and rolled a spliff expertly. At the same time while the joint was being rolled their self appointed barman readied the drinks by halving the two litre coldrink, topped it off with the entire 750ml brandy and then he shook the container until the most of the fizz had dissipated. Whilst waiting for the main course, one of the other guys lit up a cigarette and began taking a few puffs and passed it around; it was as if he was giving his arm and muscles some exercise for the forthcoming major events. When the cigarette came to Fezile, it was almost at the end and the filter was squashed and moist from the combination of saliva and heat. He had been observing how the guys had calmly taken long drags from the stick and he figured that he should follow in the same vein. Looking at Sandile who seemed just as comfortable in these surroundings as all the rest he lifted the smouldering stick to his lips and pouted as he first felt the moisture and then pulled. The smoke went in all sorts of directions in his mouth and down his throat but it was the irritation in his lungs that caused him to sputter and cough chokingly as his body rejected the gases. There were roars of laughter and sneers at his attempt to join the club but not wanting to be outdone and to suppress the headache, he drew another puff but this time he was talked through the experience and though the inhalation still burned and stung his mouth and throat, he persisted: he had to fit in and he wanted to cure the headache. He was told to hold his breath for a couple of seconds to allow the smoke to blend in with his chest and for his body to acclimatise to the polluted air and when he was ready to let the excess smoke out, he should do it slowly so that it would not run amuck on its way out. His eyes swelled, filled with tears and became red and he felt his breath becoming extremely short and he finally exhaled as instructed. The exhalation was followed by two more sputters and cheers of congratulations that he had faired better on that attempt. The sharp bitter taste of nicotine on his tongue camouflaged the pounding of the headache and he believed that it was going away, so he took a third and final hit of the stompie and his body began to relax.

He was offered some coldrink to wash down the taste in his mouth and after taking a swig, he could not even taste the sweetness of the drink so he called for the mixed bottle. He did not know what to expect from there but he knew that there was no turning back from where he had started and somewhere in his mind he heard a voice, almost like his mother's, pleading with him asking him what his father would say if he saw him drinking and smoking with those boys. It was just that, the thought of his father that made him resolute in going through with the gulp of the brandy; the anger welled up inside and he held that bottle up like it was a water bottle. At first the other boys cheered him on for his machismo but then squealed that he was finishing the booze and they pounced at him and as they pulled it away, some trickled down his cheeks and as he was catching his breath and fighting the sharp, yet sweetened taste of the burning brandy, he gasped and wiped the aqua vitae and lapping and smacking his lips. The taste was definitely something that he had never had before not even castor oil could top the sharpness and burning sensation but the anger of his father's infidelity made the taste palatable and left him wanting more. The tone from the other chaps had turned from being of cheering to disapproval because he had almost finished the booze and split some, one or two seemed to be concerned as to where that drinking appetite came from but Sandile offered that it was just stress; plain old teen and exam stress.

It was almost eleven when the first joint was ready to be fired up and shared and they made sure that they explained the rules of engagement to everyone: the spliff was not one man's girl-friend, so there was no kissing of the tip or hogging allowed; each man had to take two puffs and then pass it on and the puffs would be followed by a swig of the booze. They all agreed focus-ing their attention on Fezile who had taken up his place next to Sandile, he just smiled a wry smile and dipped his head a bit, feeling the burning brandy as it still made its way down to his colon. When the laced dope reached him he raised his head and listened to the tips on how to inhale; they were the same as the ones for the cigarette but because some of the other guys were also coughing after their hits, he proceeded with caution. He dragged slowly and allowed the smoke to fill his mouth first and then released it into his throat and down to his lungs; surpris-ingly he did not sputter out and so he went for his second hit and repeated the procedure. He found that the longer he held his breath, the easier it was to control the smoke. He finally let it out but easily as he was being coached along. Within a matter of seconds he started to feel lightheaded, even lighter than he felt after the cigarette and the tranquillity and sedation followed. The bottle of brandy came along and he raised it to his lips but this time the smell seemed sharper and he winced and sipped long enough to get that sharp burning in his mouth again and then let the bottle down to pass it along. He was given a cigar-ette but he couldn't understand why he couldn't get it in line with his mouth; he pouted to accept the butt into his mouth but whenever his hand came closer to his mouth the cigarette seemed to vanish. He tried several times to aim for the big hole under his nostrils but the damn cigarette kept on evading the gaping hole and out of exasperation, he tried to lean forward to meet up with the glowing stick but with no luck and he toppled out of his seat and would have landed face first if Sandile hadn't caught him and set him upright again. By then the other guys were in stitches at the sight of what was happening, though some of them were also having their moments of discomposure. When he managed to move his attention from the disobedient cigarette, Fezile looked at his mates and started giggling as he tried to focus on each one, by then they began looking like cartoons and as he panned across the gathering, he began laughing louder and hysterically. The more the laughter went on, the happier he felt; a type of happiness that he had never, ever felt before. He was euphoric and anything and everything that was said, was accepted with hilarity. His body began to feel heavier and his speech so incoherent that each time he opened his mouth to speak his tongue betrayed him; the sentences seemed perfectly formulated in his mind but the execution was just hopeless. Finally he gave up because every effort was taking the last bit of energy that he had and he slouched and the lights went out as his head tumbled towards the ground.

The dryness of his uvula and hard scratching sensation on his throat as he tried to swallow woke him up and as his eyes tried to focus the blur, the crimson evening sky seemed somewhat merciful to them. He covered his eyes a bit to adjust to the light and tilted his head to the side and got a glimpse Sandile who was lying in a foetal position spooning a stick with copious amounts of drool dribbling from the corner of his mouth. He wanted to lift his head but it felt like someone had weighted it down with an extremely large object; it wasn't throbbing or pounding, just buzzing incessantly. He closed his mouth trying to salivate it but when the dry air just seemed to inflict pain, he coughed. His stomach growled something fierce from the hunger and he tried to recall where he was and what had happened but he was drawing blanks. He looked around and though there was evidence that there were other people, they were nowhere to be seen. With a lot of wobbliness, he made it to Sandile and woke him up. He barely made it to his feet and as soon as he got upright, he started to feel the nausea again and his knees were completely jelly. Sandile was still protesting to being woken up from his slumber when he was beginning to shake the cobwebs when a train came rumbling along and its sound was so amplified that it felt like he had his ear on the tracks. They dusted themselves off, picked up their bags and began their journey home. Along the way they were coming up the most inventive stories to tell their parents about their appearance. Some versions involved being robbed whilst another had them being kidnapped and they had barely escaped. When Fezile got home, he had a glimmer of hope when he didn't hear the dreaded jazz and the front door was closed, so he went to the back and stealthily made his way to the door. It was wide open and he carefully peered in and listened to the voices; it was only his brother and sister's that he could make out. He ventured forth and entered, making a dash for the his bedroom and as quickly as his body would allow him, he stripped down to his draws and when he heard footsteps he kicked the dirty clothes under the bed and picked up a facecloth to wipe off the dust from his head. His sister walked in was startled by his sudden appearance, he reacted as Shinga would and demanded that she should knock or announce herself before entering a room. It was a rather bizarre command because it was after all their room and they had free access to it. When that excitement died down he enquired where their parents were and she told him that their father got called out to work due to a shortage of drivers and that he would be out of town for sometime as usual and their mom hadn't arrived as yet. A great sense of relief came over him and he got the lucky break that he needed to straighten himself out and get into bed.

The following day at school he met up with the guys and in a clandestine manner they reminisced over the previous day's session but most of it was a blur to Fezile. He was shaking like a leaf and still felt the nausea but with no pressing urge to throw up. According to the experts, it was a hangover and it would soon subside but bit of knowledge also came with all forms counsel on how to handle the shakes. There were quite a few bi-

zarre suggestions in the mix; some of which included the inges-
tion of raw foods like eggs whilst others leaned more towards a
heavy liquid intake. Some kid said that the sure fire way to get
rid of a hangover was to consume whatever it was that caused
the hangover in the first place, like whatever the alcohol taken
to cause the hangover. The guys with the stronger stomachs and
experience suggested that a kassie breakfast would be the best
thing to settle the jitters. A kassie breakfast comprised of amag-
winya (fat-cakes, the South African cousin of the doughnut
but with the centre filled in), mangola (polony), snoek-fish and
atchaar; there had to be atchaar and the spicier it is the better
it is a cure for the babalaas and besides no self respecting meal
can be called a kassie meal without atchaar and the final stroke
of a kassie meal had to be a two litre bottle of ice cold cola or a
ngolo-ngolo (a 750 ml beer) to help with the belching.

The boys had their breakfast and then headed behind the
school toilets, the smokers' spot for a postprandial relaxation;
they rolled a spliff and had a good giggle about the previous day.
They got too relaxed and seemingly forgot themselves but they
were soon brought back to their senses by the stern authorita-
tive voice that demanded that everyone remain in their current
position. The voice was met with a scuffle as the young perpet-
rators bolted in an array of directions, two of the boys charged
towards the man and as the dodged past him, one on his left and
another on his right, they knocked him off balance and he was
soon on his back. Whilst a few of the other boys were able to escape through a hole in the fence but Fezile was not so lucky as he
sat between the wall and the fence. By the time he found his
bearings and could started off on his run, the fallen policeman
was back on his feet and he lunged towards Fezile, who was un-
aware at the time that he still had the joint in his hand. The cop
didn't have to struggle much to apprehend Fezile and he soon
had him by his waist belt when another cop came through to
offer assistance. At the same spot where Fezile was nabbed,
there was a stash of dagga which one of the other boys had

dropped when they were making their getaway, so it seemed like he had dropped because he was standing over it. The police picked up the evidence and when they searched him, they found the painkillers in his pocket and that just exacerbated the situation. The cops took him to the front where there was a swarm of cops in the school grounds; it was an all out raid on the school and at each that Fezile looked at, there was some pupil being thrown in, some were protesting violently to get into the vans whilst others were being cooperative but only just so that they would not get the apartheid treatment that they had seen so many times on the telly. The principal and some of the teachers were out yelling and screaming at the some of the higher ranking cops and demanding that all the children should be released into their custody and once all the parents had been notified they could then follow up and pick the children up from their homes. The police were not even willing to listen to any reason and they continued to fill their trucks and vans, ushering some children from the classrooms and various locales around the school. Almost an hour and half later, with four trucks and six vans full, the police left a highly volatile mob of angry, chanting pupils, screaming teachers and parents, some crying as if there mourning. The convoy roared as it took its haul to the police station to begin processing the young offenders for the justice department. The charges varied for each but most were in the range of narcotics, either possession or distribution thereof.

By the time Ma-Shinga arrived at the police station, the other parents that were in attendance protested to the accusations and charges that were brought up against their children. Some just begged and pleaded that they free them because in their parental view there must have been a mistake in all that had happened. Some parents were adamant that the police had wrongfully arrested their little darlings and were threatening with lawsuits. Frantic calls were being made and every once in a while a phone was being forced on to the ear of a non compliant police officer to speak to most probably a lawyer, legally knowledgeable relative or a police officer who had some relation with the young perp. Whilst others were being forceful in their approach towards the police, there were those who knew and realised that taking a more submissive approach would be the only way to get through to the cops and then they would stand a better chance to appeal to the cops' better and hopefully parental nature to persuade them to be lenient on their child. One thing was certain; not one of those parents wanted to let their child spend the night in jail, some were even willing to exchange places for their spawn. There were a lot of devastated parents in that police station and none would believe that any of their children could be involved in drugs to the extent that the police had to crackdown so hard on the school.

As the night set in and the police station got calmer, more and more facts were coming out as each present parent went in to hear for themselves when their child was being interrogated, charged and released into their custody. When it came to Fezile's turn and he was brought in from one of the rooms where the kids were held; he recalled what some of the kids that came back had said. The experts and some repeat offenders were giving hushed talks and suggestions of denial, they were telling the other kids the loopholes of the justice system as far as kids were concerned. He walked into the interrogation room and his eyes sank as he saw his mother. He was ordered to take a seat next to his mother and then the grilling began. Initially he denied everything, he denied being in the presence of dagga smoking kids, he denied being in possession of dagga when he was arrested and he definitely denied being in possession of mandrax. His denial just seemed to infuriate the cops even further and they resorted to bringing out some chemical testers and at first he did not object as he thought that there was no way that they could detect that he had been smoking a joint - well that was what the experts in the other room told him but when the cops told him that cannabis had a nasty habit of being in the blood and urine for months at a time, his lips became pale as the blood withdrew from his face but he continued to maintain his innocence. One of the cops called for the testing equipment to be brought to their room and within half an hour, a young woman and two burly constables entered the room. The young lady had a silver suitcase similar to the one DJ's carry and when she opened it there were a whole assortment of vials and test tubes and hypodermic syringes. First she asked for his hand and she sprayed it with a transparent sweet smelling, oily liquid and as she did so, she explained to him and his mom that if Fezile had been in prolonged contact with dagga, the THC (delta-9-tetrahydrocannabinol) would show up on his skin by discolouring the areas where there were prolonged exposure. That was the beginning of the end of Fezile's charade as it took less than two minutes for his hands and finger tips to discolour; his game was up and he had less of a chance to convince them that he knew nothing about the mandrax tablets that were in his painkiller vial. To the cops, this child was definitely a habitual user and probably a runner for one of the gangs. He couldn't offer any plausible defence and the cops added fuel to the fire when they told him that the other kids had fingered him as their supplier. Sure he supplied them but it was only painkillers and not dagga and mandrax as the cops were suggesting. After seeing the results of the initial test for herself, a thoroughly disappointed and disillusioned Ma-Shinga instructed her son to cooperate and he had to give his arm for the young pathologist to draw blood which would be taken to the lab for further tests. It had been a gruelling two hours since he stepped in that room with the cops and his mother and at the end of it all he confessed to smoking a joint prior to his arrest and on the previous day but not being in possession of mandrax, he made it clear that he had painkillers on him which he got from his father but by then his attempts to clear his name fell on deaf ears. It was his initial denial of any involvement in the activities that made the police hard-hearted; in their view, he was taking them for a ride, making fools out of them and so they wanted to teach him an unforgettable lesson and make an example out the arrest. In the mix of it all, it came out from one of the cops that Fezile's school had always been under observation by a task team for several months. There had been reports of not only drug usage but selling as well from the school. Due to circumstances beyond his control and frustration, Fezile got caught for a crime that he never really intended to commit.

He was released into his mother's custody and told to be at court the following day where the case was reminded for further investigation and he was given a new date to return to court for the full hearing three months later. On that day there were a lot of disappointed parents who shared their interrogation room experience and humiliation because of their children. The very parents that were cocksure and adamant that their children were not junkies, were silenced whilst others did not even bother to take the day off to attend to their children's hearing because they were infuriated. They figured that if their kids were old enough to use drugs then they were old enough to fend for themselves against the justice system and unfortunately the magistrate ruled that they had to be present for their children's hearings, he said that it was that type of parental disregard that led the children to end up in wayward lifestyles. That magistrate gave the absent parents the riot act and was a couple of sentences shy of throwing the whole damn book at them too. He managed to scare even the parents that were there and as far as he could he pushed to settle the case there and then. The ones that managed to escape his wrath but only just were the one like Fezile who had to wait for evidence and reports to return from the forensic labs and pathologists. According to that man the parents were to blame for this decay in their children's moral fibre; in each case that was brought before him he wanted to know what the relationship between the children and parents was like and he was especially interested in the face time that the parents spent together with their children, moreover the child that was standing in his court and being asked to defend the drug related charges. Where he discovered that there was little or no face time with the child he exploded and then he would rule that both the parents and child should go for counselling and report back to his court in six months. That man had had enough of child offenders and he was determined to make examples out of the lot of those cases. At one point he stated that none of his staff would go home until the entire case pile had been cleared and he had heard every one of the drug cases related to that school, that was tough but at least it was reassuring because there were also other serious charges, such as concealed weapons, possession of stolen merchandise, possession of counterfeit material (including currency - local and international) and fortunately his court was assigned the drug cases only. It was only at the courts that the parents realised that their kids' schools were fraught with criminality and they were gobsmacked when they were hearing the range of the charges and number of repeat offenders that were there. A lot of the parents could not even look at each other partly because their child had accused the other's child or blamed them for their involvement in those activities that they were being charged for and thus they had to unwillingly rat their friends out at the insistence of their parents. In some instances, some parents had to be peeled off each other as they had gone into full on fisticuffs. Outside the courthouse the chanting masses that had accumulated since that morning to protest against the alleged abuse of power by the police had dwindled as more and more kids were being released and the fact were become clearer, as far as the courts were concerned. Their loud screams were reduced to sheepish whimpers by lunchtime and down to a deafening silence by the end of the day. Most of those kids who their communities thought of as precious little angels were as guilty as sin and they made complete and utter fools of the community members.

In the three months since his arrest, Fezile battled even further with his sanity as his mind kept on switching between his father's homosexual affair, his drug charges, the lack of trust that had been created in his family and he had no one to talk to because he had been seriously grounded after his father had given him a flogging of note. After that he cared less what happened to him and whenever the opportunity availed itself, he took off to the place where he got his cherry high and lit up just so that he could escape the hardship of his reality, he took these respites when he knew that his father would be at home for a couple of days because he really did not want to speak or look at that man. By the time they returned for the hearing, the pathology and forensic reports were led as evidence attested to the fact that the tablets in his possession at the time of his arrest were in actual fact prescription medication but that did not let him off the hook as the script was not his. The court found him guilty on the possession charge and he would have received a suspended sentence of six months but because he was high at the time of the hearing he got nine months in a juvenile rehabilitation clinic. Those nine months in rehab were to be the first lessons of his real street education because in there he learned how to beat the system and the continuous drug tests and by the time he got out, he resented his father more than ever and blamed him for the bad turn in his life. Two months after his reintegration to society, he became a regular at Mojalefa's and soon became a runner and a small time dealer at school and every so often he would be stopped and searched by the police but they always came up empty on their searches and it was during this time that the name 'Snyman' was bestowed upon him. On one unfortunate day he got arrested for housebreaking, a crime he normally did not part-take in but because he had come up short on one of his runs he had to make up for the shortage and in order to do so he had an option of housebreaking or carjacking and he opted for the former. Due to the fact that there were illegal firearms involved in the break-in, though he was never in possession of any and the fact that he had been previously fond guilty of another crime he received a harsher sentence of a year and this time he was sent straight to juvie hall. His mother had to once again attend to his legal appearances and was forced to watch as her oldest slipped out of her reach. When he came out, he was banned from the family home because his father wanted nothing to do with him and he was fine with because according to Snyman, that rotten bastard was the reason why he had turned out that way.

Inside juvie hall things were really tough, a lot tougher than the rehab clinic. He learnt that in order to survive in there he had to have some allegiance or affiliation to a gang otherwise he was just a minnow waiting to be gulped by the big fish in there. He chose or rather was chosen by the 3SG (three star gang) who got their name from the knives that they wielded, this kids were notorious for their knife tactics and they were not afraid to use their blades and being incarcerated a knife skill was far more advantageous than a gun skill. His allegiance to 3SG became possible because he could score narcs for the gang members inside and he knew where the better stash was for the guys on the outside to get their hands on and sell. It was through him and his cunning that 3SG became a noticeable drug enterprise.

THE ROGUES

Between the beating of note from a cop and being left in the company of a habitual criminal who's had serious daddy issues, I was not sure which was worse but I was a tad concerned and could only pray that he didn't get the urge to let out his frustrations, sexual or otherwise, in the immediate future. The time I lay there in his presence moved by so slowly and my nervousness welled up inside that my urges needed to be met, especially the urge to urinate but I couldn't just get up and stroll over to the pisspot so I did what anyone in my predicament would do; I let it out. In that moonlit courtyard on that hard concrete, the warm liquid just gushed out and I felt most of my pants from my thighs downward getting wet. The fluid must have reached Snyman because all I heard was:

'Ja bliksem, u ya cama masimb' ako?' (You asinine, you're peeing yourself?)

'Gimme a break you asshole, I've been swigging sorghum beer and whiskey earlier on and where do you think it was going to end up?', I thought to myself.

He got up and moved to another part of the courtyard a little bit more upwind where he started thinking aloud.

'Le two le fanele ngi ngay' jute manje, nie so ngizo hlala hier and la mabanditi ase ndlu nkulu azo ngifakel' i jive, strong!' (I mustn't cross these two now otherwise I'm going to be stuck here and those inmates at the big house WILL make my life extremely difficult!)

'iHalf-klipa sgodo yona ngay' tolla for sho, i shandis ku ngaba uku kipha le stolment se 10. Eish, maar i kgomsha fanele l'enze njane? Maar net solank anga phuma hier!' (Fifty thousand I can certainly get hold of, my problem could be the monthly ten thousand instalment. What's a hustler to do? Anyway just as long as I can get out of here!).

'Ey! Mampara! It's your lucky night. Your dossier had not yet been capture on the system but it had been assigned to an investigating officer and it should be ready for him to collect it in the morning when he starts, so it seems like we have a little bit time to play around with it.'

'Ah! Thanks Vader!'

'Let's go! We'll have to do some credible touch up artwork on the charge sheet; minor things really but they would delay the case in your favour and if you have a smart lawyer, as I am sure that you do, he will do his part to get it thrown out of court. In the meantime, you'll be out on bail and we'll all be earning a living. Right?!? Has the other cop returned with your phone?'

'Sho Vader. No Vader!'

'Ayi ke then we'll wait for him first! You can make the call and while the money is on its way, we'll work.'

'Sho that's fair Vader'.

Within moments Mokone arrived with the phone and by his standards and commentary, it was a real fancy piece of technology and decor. It was a custom made, ice studded smart phone, with a touch screen and video call capabilities; Mokone asked Snyman to confirm if the model number of the handset that he had in his hand was really Snyman's and if the ice on it were real diamonds, so much for him being a smart cop. He knew that the phone was his because he was the one that logged it in with the prisoner's personal belongings but he asked him all the same. Like a little child accepting candy or a toy from an adult, Snyman reached out his cusped hands, curtseyed and as soon as the phone came to life, he made a desperate call. The silence of our courtyard made it easy for me to hear the recipient's end of the call and initially Snyman had to resort to shouting to get this person out of the extremely noisy place, probably a club or shebeen. Although it was highly unlikely that anyone would hear the shouting that was going on in our conference room and even if they heard it, they wouldn't make out what was being said through those thick concrete walls, Mabitla ordered Snyman to lower his voice and with a great deal of difficulty, he managed to get the listener to move to a quieter place where he then updated them, in a more hushed tone, on the current developments, he issued them with instructions as to where they would find the money and what they needed to do to get him out of there.

The meeting for the pay off was set for later that morning still in the early hours but before their shift ended, Mabitla would go and meet with the suspect's source, just as he had done on many other occasions. He made sure that they scheduled to meet at the most obvious of places, the road side on his patrol route. It was a rather simple and yet effective MO (modus operandi): Mabitla would approach the car that would seemingly be parked along the road waiting for roadside assistance. The person doing the drop off would be instructed to leave the boot, hood and passenger door open and if there were to be more than two occupants in the meet, the others have to be seated on the curb side behind the car. He would then stop to offer assistance and do a supposedly routine check on the car and the occupants would be searched and questioned and during the search, usually when the rookie or partner has his head stuck into the boot or hood of the car checking the VIN (vehicle identification number), Mabitla would establish the whereabouts of his money and then nonchalantly get acquainted with it whilst circling the car in the usual policeman-like, predatory manner. Unlike the movies there are no shiny metallic briefcases or attaché cases or backpacks, those are suspicion and attract too much attention. In actual fact an amount like R50 000 is just 25 packs of a bundle of 10 single R200 notes or 50 packs of a bundle of 10 single R100 notes or a 100 packs of a bundle of 10 single R50 notes, all of which can be packed into a carton of cigarettes or fried chicken box or a 750ml whiskey box. The type of gifts that a hard working policeman deserves and likes whilst he's on the beat. On an official basis, those type of searches and routine checks yield nothing so they would not even get radioed in or noted on their occurrence books but should an overzealous rookie want to jot it down, they were welcome to do so but most of the time Mabitla would distract them before they even got the chance to pull out their book. He knew that if they did get a chance to write them up, they could oneday catch up with him, so the best thing was to skilfully deter the young ones from colouring in their books, as required by law.

Once the money had been picked up, he would drive around his route for another ten minutes or so and then return to the police station where he would transfer the money to his car before he headed into the charge office. It was all inconspicuously done and no one would ever even think of checking on his movements or what he was carrying, he was after all a respectable commissioned officer in the police services and a good family man.

Mokone had told his deckhand that he was going for a walkabout and a smoke, so that itself removed all suspicion from his lengthy disappearance from his station. When Mabitla returned to the police station, Mokone and Snyman were chatting, smoking and having a hearty drink, as if they were long time acquaintances and in the meantime I lay there on the cold concrete floor in a freezing puddle of urine and every once in a while I would grunt and fart just to get their attention in the hope that they would drag me into cell but they would just burst out in vulgarity and laughter and continue with their camp stories. The two men were definitely on opposite sides of the law but for those minutes that they spent together, they were just a couple of guys having a good old chin-wag. This was the beginning of a relationship but there wouldn't be any braais and baptismals, weddings and other socials and so forth just a thirty second meet, greet and exchange of packages. During those few minutes they touched up, ever so briefly, on their backgrounds, their old and new dreams and aspirations. They did not dwell on the intricacies of their current jobs, probably in fear of selling each other out and ruining their cash cows but they did share with each other how they both ended up in their career paths and the one thing that was a thread common to both the men was that if they could do it all over again, they would have done it differently. They would have chosen less dangerous and health hazardous careers; Snyman said he would have been an IT specialist and Mokone said that he would have liked to have been a chorister. When he was still in school, he enjoyed being in the choir and his choir master was a very supportive tutor and he could even get a crow to sing in harmony but his mother constantly discouraged him, telling him that there was no money and future in that sort of thing. After numerous failed attempts from his tutor to convince his mother that her son had a talent he lost hope and after school he tried his hand at various odd jobs but found no joy there until he joined the police services at the insistence of his uncle.

Mabitla entered and broke up the scene with the good news that he and Mokone were R50 000 richer and that all the paperwork had been handled accordingly. He reached out his hand and took over the whiskey that the two men had been sharing and began explaining to Snyman once again how he had doctored the charge sheet so that when the matter was being brought to court it would be disputed not because of the charges but because of incorrect identity. The fingerprints would not match the ID number or the name so it would be a case of mistaken identity on the part of the state and he would walk out scot free from the court. The probability of the case being further investigated and brought back to court would be minimal as the case loads for the detectives in their corner of the woods were incredibly high. The docket would be brought back to the constabulary where it would accumulate dust on the detectives desk and then he would every once in a while jot some notes stating that he has made some attempt to locate the suspect or is still waiting for correct information from Tshwane and other agencies and finally he would close the case as unsolved due to lack of information. In certain cases there were inquiries that were opened and investigation held to check on the arresting officers and the detectives but that was not their problem. They were there to help the community and as far as this case was concerned, Snyman was part of their community. The sad and unjust part of their business was that a number of honest cops had taken the fall for their unscrupulous deeds, many shields had been bent and burned because of them but they didn't care, as long as their end of the law was kept all was fine. He also made sure that Snyman, as he had done with the others under his protective shakedown fold, was aware of the fact that the real charge sheet was in a safe place and should he ever have any thoughts on reneging on their deal then the case would be re-opened and this time everything would be in place as it was supposed to have been.

Mokone cuffed and shuffled Snyman back to his original cell, whilst Mabitla went to get him his money. They returned once again to my humble abode and concluded the transaction. Mabitla told Mokone to take the copy of the original charge and stash it with the other ones that they had stashed; again which was in plain sight. They were all placed in the prisoners' belongings safe under the guise of some non existent prisoner's personal effects. No one cared to look there because not many officers wanted to consort with the prisoners or the lock up and it was hardly ever cleaned out thoroughly.

The shift came to an end and no one was ever happier than me. The final cell check was done and it was during that time that Mokone came in and gave me a jolting wake up with a cold bucket of water. He prodded me a couple of times with a mop stick that he brought in and told me to clean up my mess and then get out of their hotel. With a stagger and a stumble, I made sure that most of the floor was covered with my vomit and urine and when he realised that things weren't going according to plan, he grabbed me by arm and led me to the lock up gate and further escorted me to the street and told me to keep walking or else he would really lock me up and throw away the key. The man did not have to say that twice because with what I had heard throughout the night, I was sure that he would do it without a second doubt and no one would even question him about it. As we walked towards the gate, the cops that had trickled in and had noticed the old gatekeeper and his prisoner, sneered and jeered at him but that didn't seem to bother him at all, as a matter of fact, it seemed as though it was habitual. Why would he mind I thought to myself, the man had just settled a deal that made him R25 000 richer and it came with a R5 000 monthly retainer.

I wanted to hug the man and thank him immensely for his copious contribution to my spadework and to ask him to thank his devoted cousin and business partner for me but I had to restrain myself and the fresh morning breeze on my wet pants was a huge and constant reminder that I had to get out the clothes that I was in. The clothes also served as a reminder that I had a long and painful walk back to the airport parking to pick up my car and to get myself home and as much as I wanted to hurry back, I could not afford to raise any suspicion by being miraculously lucid and walking like a member of the rat-race. I began my trek back to the airport, fighting back every attempt that I was making not to fiddle around with the surveillance equipment and the gestures of me slapping my hand away from my chest every time it sneaked up or touched any of the equipment must have been a bizarre sight to any passer-by but it did keep me entertained through most of the journey.

THE CLEANER

With the knowledge that I had acquired courtesy of SM&M (Snyman, Mabitla and Mokone) Enterprises I needed to rethink and enhance my next move, in a way, I needed to change my tactics a tad so that I could widen the ambit of the project. I had been recently unjustly accused of a crime that I had not committed nor even thought about committing but I had just spent a couple of hours in the vicinity of someone who openly admitted to committing a similar crime, repeatedly at that and he was going to allowed to roam the streets freely and get the protection of the very same people who were legally bound to stop him from proliferating his business. The thought of this further enraged me and as I reviewed the blurry lock up footage and muffled sound bytes, the more I felt compelled to bring down as many of these rogue cops as possible but this was not without the frustrating thought and knowledge that I could not put a complete stop to that cancer and what was even more frustrating was that I would require much more information and resources than what I had but I was sure that along with Ashwipe, Judas and their merry band of rogues that came to visit me, SM&M had to be shut down one way or another.

I didn't want to go into this half-cocked so as part of my intense research, I solicited the counsel of some legal experts and also recalled what both Tobey and Alwyn had said regarding my raid and raids in general. It was striking how similar all the unofficial testimonials of the police officers that I spoke to confirmed that that such a raid was absurd and illegal and that it was highly probable that it was supposed to be a hit. Some even said that God was definitely on my side because one of three things were supposed to happen: I was either supposed to get convicted, which would ruin me socially for a long time or I was supposed to get killed in those holding cells or get killed during the raid.

It was clear that the raid was not only illegal in the sense that they did not have the authority to conduct their search, seizure and arrest; it was also improper, poorly conducted and not done within standard police operating procedures. It also came to light that, in order for a search to be done, there had to be a reason or motive and in my case it should have been the suspicion of handling and dealing of banned narcotics from my premises. This would have led to a case being built where a task team would have been assembled to investigate and report back through the proper chain of command. Once they had collected sufficient evidence during their investigation, including floor plans of the premises they had intended to search, they would then have had to apply for a search warrant from a court and that warrant would state exactly where they had intended to search, showing specifically where they were going to conduct their search; that meant that if their intel had led them to believe that the drugs were kept under a bed then they would have had to confine their search to that particular area. After acquiring their warrant they would have had the option of approaching the local precinct to get back up and that could have been done on the day or just a few hours before the raid. However, the matter of liaison with the local precinct would have been done carefully and strategically in the event that one of the local police were working with the suspects. The search party would then be deployed and would have been consisting of dog units, chemical testing equipment, forensic experts (where and when available), latex gloves and forensic bags; so that they would not taint the evidence being collected. Upon arrival at the premises, they would have had to ensure that they covered all the doors and windows so that any chances of escape for the suspects would be minimised. The owner or occupants of the premises would be identified and served with the warrants which would clearly outline the reasons that the police were there for and then the search would proceed. Each item which would have been deemed suspicious would have been interrogated and bagged in the forensic plastic bag and the bag would then be sealed. Each bag has a unique number for record purposes and the bags themselves are made of a clear toughened plastic, not like a garbage disposable bag and the seals are an adhesive type at the opening of the bag, so once the bag has been sealed it cannot be easily re-opened without damaging the bag. Once sealed, the bag would be logged and then loaded into one of the cars designated for the collection of evidence. The suspect, before being cuffed and carted away would be shown all the collected evidence and would sign a document that the evidence collected was in fact the evidence that was taken from their premises and possession. Though the process may seem long, tedious and extremely labour intensive but when it is done properly, the probability of a conviction is near total. Every time I heard the procedure, I played out the events of 05 March 2010 in my head and I tagged the flaws and I lost count or maybe I just stopped counting after fifteen faults because my head would buzz and the anger would well up to the point that I would lose focus and almost blackout.

I discovered that, in essence, I had an easy task which was to undo all that these cops had done and that meant mirroring their work and though I would not have full access to all their resources, offices and labs, I had to do the best with what I could lay my hands on. I found sufficient clues for me to work on but in order to succeed, I needed to factualise them and correlate activities to specific people. I had started at the right place, the lock up and that, in itself opened up a whole new avenue. The next step was to lay my hands on the paperwork and I was convinced that the investigating officer, Molwedi, could and would be of great assistance but unfortunately, it would not be feasible to just knock on his office door and play twenty questions with him, however if I went in under the guise of a familiar, yet unobtrusive, individual I could inconspicuously allow myself access into his and as many offices as possible or required. Then I remembered that in large organisations, nobody really remembers the cleaners; they are the custodians of dirt and as such are rarely socialised with. In most cases, those in the higher echelons of the organisations are unlikely to have a fully fledged conversation that would go beyond some sort of courteous greeting and possibly an enquiry about how much longer they will invading their work space with their cleaning duties. To organisation members, cleaners are part of the faceless society, they exist but who cares who they are or where they come from or what their dreams and aspirations are; they are just cleaners, people who are there to tidy up after the more privileged and prominent members of society. They would only be remembered when the conduciveness of the environment does not suit the privileged or when something goes missing then they are part of the initial suspects. I decided that I was going to obtain my information illegally and though the thought bothered me initially, I recalled that because I had done things by the book as was taught an preached to all my life, the damn thing was nearly thrown at me, so I was going to play by these alternate rules and like in many sports, if the referee does not see it, it is deemed legit or unrefereed and thus does not interfere with the play.

From my initial stakeouts of the station, I had noted that the office cleaning was outsourced to a cleaning company and their van would come by and drop off staff and cleaning supplies. I opted to follow up on them and use them as my entry into the police station so I did an online search for their details and found out that it was a small local business which was privately owned by two women, probably housewives and like most small businesses in the Kempton Park, they were operating it from a suburban house in the west. Vuk'uzenzele (Get up and do it for yourself) was a woman's only gig and by reading trough the website it seemed more and more that the prospects of me getting employment there to gain access to the police station were minimal. If I was fortunate enough the most I could get was a job as their gardener or security guard but not as part of the general cleaning crew. It felt like I had hit an impasse because of all the strategies of gaining access to the SAPS, this was the lowest of all the low key options but I couldn't afford to abort this mission, it was too important, the information that had to be obtained inside was too valuable for my quest for justice and above everything else my anger was not ready to forgive me or my accusers, so I had to find a way to make the plan work. The frustration of seeing the target and knowing that it was achievable yet not being able to execute the first phase of the operation was mounting up and I was beginning to feel helpless. I thought of getting some outside help, maybe one of my female relatives that needed a job but then recalled that such a delicate assignment needed the utmost discretion and it could not be entrusted to just anyone. The other challenge that would arise regarding outsourcing that type of mission was the fact that Nthabi would have been mortified to know that I would have trusted another woman more than her and then there was the element of danger for the aide; should she get caught the ramifications would be far reaching and I did not want to have that weight to bear.

Instead of moping around and losing hope I headed out to Vuk'uzenzele just to see the place and there could be a slim possibility that I could find another lead to proceed with the plan, after all there was nothing else to lose. The house where Vuk'uzenzele was operating from was situated in an area which had had more than its fair share of suburban crime and was the fifth house from the corner and two streets away from the main road, which meant that it was easily accessible by private car but for someone using public transport it was a bit of a schlep. Their security comprised of the usual: an electric fence, an intercom on an automated gate, which oddly enough was ajar, an alarm, which was probably connected to an armed response company and burglar bars on the windows. It was all pretty standard, nothing out of the norm like a moat with starved alligators and piranhas or thermal infrared cameras on the perimeter fence and house walls - just average security for an average home or small business. I parked on the street along the high fence and pulled out a clipboard and lab coat from the boot and walked into the yard, expecting someone to come out from the back or from the front door of the purple with lime trimming house to stop my advances but I made it uninterrupted to the door and even as I stood at the open doorway for a couple of seconds scanning my immediate environment before alerting the receptionist with my entry, I kept a wary sense about me. The office-like reception area showed signs of refurbishment, it seemed like it was where it was once the dining room of the house, it had shiny wooden floors and a strong smell of pot-pourri but not like the one that came from cleaning agents that were readily attainable from the local supermarket, and this was industrial strength smell. To the immediate right of the door there were two steps leading down to the reception room itself and again it had tell tale signs of conversion from residential to commercial usage, the furniture in there, for starters, was neither official nor domestic, it gave the room the feeling that a great effort was made into making it homely in the professional sense. The reception desk which was right across from the door where I was still standing, was attended to by a twenty-something year old lady who was quite absorbed by pictures on the supersized computer screen and that was evident by the continuous clicking of the mouse and the way she clicked faster in an attempt to remove the pictures from the screen when she caught sight of me with my hand feigning to knock on the door. She took another look at me and acknowledged my presence and continued to clear her screen as she greeted and invited me in. I approached her desk and quickly scanned her desk for anything that I might find useful and asked her if I was in fact the right place for my delivery, it was the first thing that came to mind when I opened my mouth when she asked me if she could help me. It turned out that she was not from around the neighbourhood and was not too familiar with the streets but she was very willing to help me so she stood up to go ask one of her colleagues in another office. As she took off, I invited myself to a seat at her desk and before she had even turned the corner my eyes laid rest on a paper with the police station name on it, it was the roster for the ladies. I didn't hesitate in acquiring it and shoving it under some of my papers on my clipboard and as I took that, I realised that the entire file for the police station lay under it, so I added that to my shopping cart as well. Her desk and the floor were a clutter, so she would not even notice that it was missing until she had to work on it again. I slid the file into my lab coat sleeve and clutched my clipboard so that it would not be evident that my one arm had a slightly bigger bulge than the other. Her footsteps on the wooden floor down the corridor were a dead giveaway that she was returning, so that gave me just enough time to compose myself because then my gut was rumbling from the anxiety and nerves. When she got back to the desk she pulled back her chair and plumped herself in it and slid into her desk, the force in which she manoeuvred was so great that her chair's armrests collided with the desk, knocking over her coffee mug which was resting on the computer box, the result of which was muffled crackling and sparks from the liquid making contact with the electrical device. Before I even had time to think, I was indiscriminately pulling out cables at the back of the computer and she hip-hopped about to the tune of the crackling sparks and during that rescue operation, my hand got hold of a flash drive that was also plugged into the box and as I pulled it out a puff of smoke rose up out the box, muscle reflex never allowed my hand to return to the box and it must have been the same reflex which clammed my hand shut with the drive in it. A woman in her early forties came rushing from one of the offices enquiring what was going on and the distraught receptionist just broke down in tears. I explained what happened and as I got to the exciting part of the coffee spilling, the young receptionist bawled even more and in effort to comfort her, her colleague took her to another room. I never even got to the end of the story and the two women had left me standing there by myself so I picked up my clipboard and with my conscience gnawing at me, I left them to each other. The imminent threat of the fire was so overwhelming that it had overpowered the anxiety and nerves that I felt earlier on. I got into the car and drove off but I could not stop thinking about how I almost destroyed Vuk'uzenzele. If I hadn't gone there, that young woman would still be innocently ogling over her pictures on the screen and not some trauma victim, as a result of my pursuit for vengeance, she would probably lose her job and her company would lose days, if not weeks or months of productivity and records. How could I have been so stupid and selfish? What was I thinking off, embarking on such a mission and how far would I have to go in order to see the job through? I really felt bad, far worse than I could have imagined. Those women probably put in their life savings to start up that business and in one fell swoop; I almost destroyed it, if I hadn't destroyed it already. When I got home, I didn't even take out the clipboard, I just took the file and dumped it on the couch and sat listlessly next to it, pondering over what had happened and if all I was doing and was about to do was really worth it. I was done in and hurt but did that give me licence to go about destroying peoples' lives or was it justifiable and in pursuit of truth and justice? Justice? I found the thought of that laughable because I had now resorted to breaking the law in order to get retribution. I found some consolation in another thought that the insurance company would pay for the damages and they would be up and running again in a short time but I could not get over the fact that if I had not gone there and had possibly taken another option, things would have turned out differently. What other option and how different, I didn't know. I was playing a movie in my head, a movie that had never been made. I needed a potent drink to readjust myself and the best that I could offer my system then was a good solid brew of coffee.

After several cups of coffee and chocolate, I stashed the file and went to pick Nthabi up from work and that evening as we dined, with the incident at Vuk'uzenzele intermittently flickering in my mind, I thought of how difficult and challenging a working woman's day must be like and how as men we never really fully grasp the amount of effort and sacrifice women actually put in. I had always listened to her tell me about her day from the time she signed on to the moment that she signed off. There were accounts about how some captains were behaving like the playground bullies and some passengers who genuinely thought that by purchasing a ticket then they were entitled to a lot more than a flight with complimentary drinks and snacks. When I was a senior manager in the industry I acknowledged the challenges that my women colleagues were having but something about that day's activities made it all sink in and really hit home. I also realised that though there were laws to make the male and female workers equal, the playing field was still far from being level and unless the attitudes of the male labour force changed, no amount of laws would ever make the terrain equitable. It was probably my partial participation in the conversation or maybe the fact that that's just how marriages work - you get to know your spouse - that made her say something about right and wrong decisions. She told me that on one of the sectors that she had flown that day, the captain had taken on more fuel than he should have and instead of defueling, as per procedure, he decided to leave behind the cargo and some baggage. If he had chosen to defuel, it would have taken much longer, ultimately the flight would have been delayed by up to three hours because they would have lost their take off slot and the subsequent delays would have seen them being out of flight and duty time which would have resulted in the last two sectors of their flight being cancelled or a standby crew being called out, which would have meant a higher cost to the company. However, with another flight being scheduled within the hour, the cargo and bags that were left behind would follow with a lesser cost to the company and the majority of the passengers would not have been inconvenienced. That pilot's momentary incompetence could have adversely affected close to two hundred passengers but because of his recovery strategy probably only five ended up being affecting and the likelihood of the matter being delved into was slim to none. I thought about that story and realised that, I was in a similar predicament and if I was going to dwell on that afternoon's incident then I might as well abandon my mission and let the bad guys win, again. All I had to do was find a way to make it up to Vuk'uzenzele, pretty much like I had done in the Customer Service Recovery department in the airline; I could do nothing about the events that led to the delay that had occurred or to the bag being short shipped but I had the power to make the passenger's next flight with the airline more pleasurable and hassle free and with that thought I parked the mishap and rechanneled my thoughts and energy to my gorgeous wife, my family and my mission.

Over the next couple weeks that followed, I took it easy, not because I wanted to but mainly because Nthabi and the kids were at home and I did not want this whole thing to consume me further than it already had. I still had a family and a life to live and I owed it to them to be a loving husband and father, they were after all my dose of sanity and I could not deprive them or myself of the wonderful blessings that we had. I immersed myself in their presence and being by doing what any other normal family did; we did homework together, played some board games and hired some movies. When the boys were at school, Nthabi and I would clean the house, do the laundry or go do some window shopping and if the weather permitted we would go to the dam and stoke up a braai for lunch. Unlike most guys, I didn't have the pressures of the office or the displeasure of having to seek the permission of a boss in order to live my life, I was a stay-home dad and a house-husband and that meant I had a lot of time on my hands. I had the privilege of being the prince that most women could only dream of having in that, I could make Nthabi's lunch and put in a loving, personal hand written message in her skaftin, I could chauffer her to and from work and when she came back from work, she could get a foot massage and before she went to bed she could a full body massage. She didn't have to cook or clean or iron, those were all my duties and I enjoyed doing them for her and the boys, though I often roped the boys in on the cooking and cleaning but that was primarily to get them to be appreciated for their efforts and exercising some of my parental rights. I was proud of what I had taught them, they displayed great culinary skills and really kept the house clean, so much so that I would sometimes feel that they were outdoing me. Even Thando contributed because he would start the day off by pulling out the broom and dusters from the closet and laying them out almost as a reminder that no toddler should play around in a dusty area but we'd end up in a disagreement when it came to mopping up the floor because he always figured that the mopping water was just as good for dunking in anything that needed cleaning, including his bottles, diapers and laundry and if he didn't or couldn't find a cloth to dip in the water to help me mop then he figured that his tiny hands would do the job just as well. Those were things that I really got to cherish and more than I realised, I had Judas and Ashwipe to thank because their injustice led me to become closer to the one thing that I had been convincing myself that I had been sacrificing for the most: my family.

At the end of the grande family time, I took Thando to my parents' place at their insistence. Officially my mom said that they wanted to help out and that they would have Thando there with them until the whole case had been shut because when those hoodlums came over, he was in the house and only a couple of months old and they were afraid that those guys would return and they wanted to have him out of harms way and that in order for me to recover, I needed some time to deal with things. Unofficially, I think my mom knew that I would not let the matter rest that easy and she didn't want Thando in harms way and in all probability, if had been with me full time, I would have just let things be and got along with my meagre existence and accepted the raid as an unjust travesty. Nonetheless, the family time was over and I got back to work on the mission and dug out the file and studied it; it furnished me with a variety of titbits from the cleaner's roster to the cleaning schedules to the cleaning chemicals needed and used at Kempton Park Police Station. The flash drive gave me even more than I had bargained for, it was truly the icing on the cake because it contained the original business proposal to the police procurement department which included the company's registration certificate from the Department of Trade and Industry, the company's accountant and details, their tax certificates, their letterheads, the list of directors, the client database and a lot of personal material. I had everything that was required for a company to be operational and from the type of information stored on the drive, it was clear that it belonged to one of the owners and if the level of company information stored on it was not testimony enough, the JPEG files surely gave it away.

I examined all the documentation, scrutinising it for reliable intel that I could use to gain my unsuspicious access to the station and correlating the rosters with the staff, I found the doorway. As I sifted through the paper trail, I also found the real history of the company. Vuk'uzenzele was originally Jagter's Veld (Hunter's Grounds) Enterprises CC and when I checked on the government company's database website, I found out that it was registered as a security, catering and training company to Mr. Daniel Francois Le Roux as the main managing member and his partners were his better half, Mrs. Yvonne Mariette Le Roux and Hendrik Frensch Malan, who turned out to be his brother-in-law. However, from the emails and copies of letters on the flash drive, there was an indication that the company had changed hands. Furthermore there were copies of MOU's (memoranda of understanding) between the Le Roux's, Malan and the current owners, Ms. Senzile Ndou and Mr. Petrus Solile Ntumantuma. The two new directors' names sounded familiar but I could not place where I had heard or seen them before, so I dismissed that as a coincidence. Ndou and Ntumantuma, according to their ID numbers, were teenagers when the company was registered but for all intense and purposes of registration of the company, they had full directorial powers. The MOU's, on the other hand, stated otherwise in that the two teens had no say in the daily running of the company nor did they have to lay out any start up capital but they would each receive a fixed monthly salary, annual bonuses and profit share at the end of the financial year. In reality that meant that the ownership of the company was still largely that of Le Roux and his family and these two were stool pigeons. That deal sounded very familiar and for that time of our lives and democracy, it was very realistic. The black directors in the company were actually there for statistical purposes or to give the company an edge to get business because it could prove that it had PDI's (previously disadvantaged individuals) and the more blacks there were on the directorship, the greater the opportunities seemed and the likelihood to get more business and government grants would double if the PDI's were women. It was unscrupulous business and black people were being used as tokens to jump the queue and acquire the lucrative corporate meal ticket, in as much as they wanted a meal as well. I, too, once took part in such a company but parted ways due to the depth of the corruption that it entailed; apart from having my name in the directorship of the company, the person who was most likely to influence the acquisition of our service wanted us to make it worth their while to get their company give us the business, so we were not going to get the business because we deserved it but because we had lined their pocket and this amount would be worked into the overall bill of their company. Here are the basics of the deal: we approach the client with the proposal and offer to do the service for them and in one of the meetings we would then establish who would be the key person to either make the final decision or influence that final decision, from there we initiate a relationship with that individual, outside the boardroom and that would entail lunches, drinks, some social events or the likes. Up until there everything was still above board and was deemed normal or within normal business practices, however, things would then take a turn at the social level because we then got to learn more about the person's individual and personal needs, which were mostly financial and those needs varied from a toy for their child to the next payment for their house and by taunting them with how much easier partnering up with our business would make their lives, we would then offer to take care of some of their personal problems and that meant having to buy the toy or give them a financial gift so that they could pay their bond. Once they got a taste of the financial freedom, they would then be able to sway the decision to take us on; after all we had shown them that we were part of their family and not just there for the sake of making money. Their acceptance of the gift would ebb away at their moral judgement and it would appeal to their self interests so that their needs were placed above their company needs. From there it would be down hill because the gifts would keep streaming in and the more they did so, the more they became dependant on them - pretty much like an addiction and all the time they were being assured that no one would ever find out. During all that wooing and courtship, the profit margins for the business venture were thrown in so that they could see that if they did accept our business, they would sit with a hefty raise and be able to self sustain their new lifestyle and in the meantime, our numbers guys were building in all these corporate gifts into the manufacturing, resources and productivity bills. In the ultimate end the decision maker or influencer would cave in and ask for a substantial off the records sign up fee to guarantee that they vote for our company and award us the business - Tendertrepreneurism 101. In the case of Vuk'uzenzele, communiqués between the SAPS procurement manager and both the previous and current directors outlined the bid and proposal for Jagter's Veld to do training and ultimately the awarding of the cleaning contract to Vuk'uzenzele and in reading in between the lines, it was clear that though this company may have been responsible for the cleaning of a police station, it's own house was very dirty and these people were nothing more than tendertrepreneurs; the newest and most venomous type of business people.

Having learnt all that, I felt much consolation about the incident at their office and got myself ready for implementing the next phase of my plan: Selina. She walked into Kempton Park Police Station on a Friday afternoon, she was going to fill in for one of the regular cleaners who was on leave and from my previous stakeouts of the place I knew that by that time, most of the gumshoes and clerks would be getting ready to leave or gone for the weekend and thus would pay very little attention to the new cleaner in their midst. She was a very low key type of person who, aside from her slightly masculine build had no striking features. She was in tracksuit pants covered by the Vuk'uzenzele uniform, with a hint of make up, some eyebrow pencil, a bit of eye shadow, lip gloss to help bring out more of her femininity to her appearance and topped off with an inexpensive feminine deodorant. She was not anything like a drag queen or cabaret dancer but someone, who at first glance and some scrutiny, could pass off as an ordinary working mom. At first, I felt really stupid and thought that I looked ridiculous when I put the disguise on but then focused on being less self conscious because I realised that if I doubted myself, then it would be harder to convince an onlooker that I was a woman and not a man trying to pose as a woman. I told myself that there were some masculine looking women in the world and that I was just one of those and fortunately for me when I was growing up, right through my teens, some people would actually address me as Miss and at first I would be really upset and complain to my mother that I don't look manly like my father and in her wisdom she would just say that when God made me, He wanted to show people that beauty was not just meant for women and that men can be beautiful too. It was hard to grapple with those words as a child but for that exercise, I was really glad that I looked a lot like my sisters and my mom and the fact that I didn't have facial hair was also a big boost. I put on a wig and a beanie to completely alter my looks and I almost didn't recognise myself when I looked at the mirror; it was like I was looking at one of my sisters in the mirror, albeit with track pants, an overall and a pair of feminine sneakers.

I was quite nervous when I entered the courtyard but I just clutched onto the handbag and lightened my gait to give it a more feminine touch and when I got one or two approving looks from passersby my confidence began to lift, though I still walked with my head slightly bent so as not to make too much direct eye contact with oncoming people. The other thing that seemed to help was that everyone was going about their own Friday business, so it was easier for me to make my way to the administrator office. The station administrator's office was manned by two women and for a moment I felt that I was going to be caught out because it was going to be a daunting task to convince them that I was the new cleaner and a woman at that but it was too late to turn back, they had seen me in the doorway. I knocked on the open door and let myself in and in a hushed voice, I greeted them, the one lady frowned disapprovingly and shot a confused look at her colleague, who at the sound of my voice stopped what she was busy with then.

'Re ka ho thusa, ausi?' (Can we help you miss?)

'Ke nna Selina, ketsoa ko Vuk'uzenzele.' (I'm Selina, I'm from Vuk'uzenzele) I continued in my hushed voice,

'Selina!?!' she exclaimed, even more confused,

'Yvonne ong rometse hore ke tlo sebetsa mmo sebakeng sa Rosina Selebakwe.' (Yvonne sent me here to work in Rosina's Selebakwe's place), I said trying not to sound too nervous and I scratched around in my bag to find an envelope.

'Rosina? O kae eena?' (Rosina? Where is she?)

'O leefing, Yvonne omphile lengoalo le hore ke lefe lona. O etse email ea bona ha e sebetse empa lengoalo lena, le tla hlalosa, hape o ka mo fonela ha ho na le ntho e o batlang ho mbotsa.' (She's on leave, Yvonne gave me this letter for you. She said her email is not working but this letter would explain and you can give her a call if there's anything else you wanted to know), I continued trying to keep my composure.

'Tjo, Tselane ong tsoarele! Rosina o la ka bua hore o tlo ea leefing maar hake hopole hore o eetse nneng.' (Forgive me Tselane. Rosina did say she was going to go on leave but I don't remember when she said she was going to go), her colleague exclaimed and joined the conversation in an apologetic manner.

Tselane was now caught between the letter from Yvonne, the confirmation from her colleague about what was happening and my appearance. The first two were easy to get past her but I had to wade in shallow waters and see what her next move was going to be regarding the woman who sat facing her and then when she picked up the phone to call Yvonne, I decide to get her to focus on me because I was not too sure how or what Yvonne would say to her on the phone. I scratched into my bag again and pulled out some items and placed them one by one on her desk; they were a small make up bag, a purse, a can of deodorant and some sanitary pads and that seemed to work as she slowed down her dialling, looked at her colleague and then again at the items on her desk and at me as I carried on excavating the handbag and finally came out with Yvonne's business card and a laminated Vuk'uzenzele personnel identification card complete with the horrible mandatory photo, birth date, worker number and the date I joined Vuk'uzenzele, which had been set to two years prior. She took the cards, scrutinized the identification card and took a long look at me and back to the card and finally dropped the phone that was cradled on her shoulder and commented on the photo.

'Motho ha a o shebile aka re o monna,' (when someone looks at you they could say that you're a man) she said as she returned the cards and I began repacking my bag.

'Ha u oa pele ho bua joalo!' (You're not the first to mention that) I said in a cold hushed voice as I continued to pack, 'Molimo omphile botle baka ke le mong!' (God gave me my own beauty), I said scathingly and she embarrassingly backed off.

'Ong tsoarele, ne ke sa buoe hampe neke fela ke sa sheba ho...' (please forgive, I didn't mean to sound so offensive, it's just that I didn't expect...)'

'...ho bona mosali o mobe je ka nna! Se kgatatsehe, se ke tloae-tse; ebile puo ea hao esale betiri, babang ha ke sa tlotsa make up ba mpitsa "abuti".' (...to see such an ugly woman like me! Don't worry, I'm used to it besides your comments are mild others have referred to me as 'sir' when I don't have make up on), I said to them both breaking the tension with a muffled smile, all the time hoping that Tselane would not go back to the phone and leave things as they were.

'Ha re ee ke lo ho bontsa mo o tlo sebeletsang teng.' (let me go show you where you'll be working), she said utterly humiliated and humbled.

Tselane showed me the offices and though some were locked because their occupants had already left, she gave me instructions for each office such as which office needed polishing and which were accessible and at which times and lastly where I could find the key for all the offices in the building. As soon as I had heard and seen where the keys were and the fact that I would have access to all the offices, I almost switched off from her tutorial. I was going to officially begin work on Monday but I convinced her that I needed the extra pay and that I could begin the following day to familiarise myself with the transport route and their office environment. She also reassured me that I was not going to report to the uniformed police personnel be-cause cleaning was considered to be part of the administrative team and with that she came across like we were going to be the best of friends while I was going to be there. Hypocrite, I thought but then so was I.

On Saturday, I dropped off the kids at my sister's place for the weekend and returned home to get Selina ready for work. Selina walked through the front door of the police station and strolled right past the empty front desk which had a handful of cops engaged in various activities: one was helping a family lodging a complaint, two were reading a newspaper, another two were chatting whilst checking through some radios and equipment and two seniors were sitting at a desk going through a heap of paperwork and signing off books. I headed to the back offices and went to the cleaner's room which was a dingy room with a mouldy ceiling, with evidence of dampness seeping through the wall, an old style table synonymous with the old regime, two dilapidated chairs, some movable lockers for the staff's personal efforts, loads of cleaning equipment on the floor and in the storage cupboards and a roster and notices on the wall. It was evident that the people that occupied that room were just placed there and very little attention was being paid to them or its contents; everyone was just too busy with their own thing to babysit a bunch of cleaners and that suited me just fine. After surveying the room a bit more, I put my things in an empty locker and like all the others there, I locked it with a small padlock and grabbed a cleaning trolley and made my way out to tend to the offices. I had to start off with Tselane's office and she had left the key at the front so I had to face the mob there but I was not going to let their unfamiliarity with my looks faze me and after a few brief sentences with them, I got the key and carried on. I had turned the corner when I heard the roar of laughter trailing behind me, obviously they remained there making fun at me but I did not care, I had more important things on my mind and for the next couple of days I knew that there were going to be some snide remarks and comments behind my back. Tselane's office was clean but I had to make sure that she knew that I had been there so I emptied her bin and purposely left it at the door instead of where I had found it, it was going to be my distinguishing mark for the offices that I had cleaned in their absence. Her computer was logged out but their filing cabinet was left unlocked so that gave me a good starting point for my intended searches; I whizzed through their files for Vuk'uzenzele files and all other businesses and whatever was of interest or noteworthy, I made notes of and where possible I removed some originals with the intention of making copies. The next office of interest to me, oddly enough, was the human resource office where I would get personnel records and that was an even more laborious task but well worth it. I got more than enough information on Mabitla, Mokone, Ntumantuma, Molwedi and Ndou but because I needed time to really go through them, I put them in a protective plastic and stuffed them into the black garbage bag on the cleaning trolley; they were going to be my homework for the evening. The last office for the day was the IT office where I was hoping to find access to the network and the various signing on codes of the key personnel and the computer was still logged on, the user did not click 'OK' to confirm log off and execute shut down procedures when they left the previous day. From there it was easy to get what I was hoping to find, I went through the network places and copied the IP addresses of the computers and there weren't that many in Kempton Park police station, most belonged to the administrative team, four were assigned to the forty or so detectives and the remaining ten were those that belonged to the commissioned officers, that was the likes of Ntumantuma and Ndou. There was a crafty little trick that I learnt from one of my many exes' on how to get into a user's computer and see what they were up to without them knowing that I had been there and through that I delved into the ten key computers. I loaded up my flash drive with files and folders of anything that was not system based, if it was end-user originated, I dumped it onto the stick; it was a real data mining filled with all sorts of gems and I would have all the time at home to carefully and leisurely go through it. The last bit of information that I sourced from the IT office were the log in and passwords for all users and at the end of it all, I left the computer the same way I found it because I realised that I would need more storage space for the information I was getting.

I was besides myself with the progress that I had made but I could not make any hasty moves and risk blowing my cover so I carried out my cleaning duties as set out for Vuk'uzenzele staff and at the end of my shift, I took my cleaning trolley back, emptied out my garbage bag, changed back into Selina's wardrobe and went to bid the front desk crowd goodbye as I left Tselane's key and headed home. It was when I got home and emptied out Selina's handbag that I appreciated women's handbags because if it was not for her guise and her large handbag, I would have had some difficulty in taking out all those files. I knew that I had only that evening to go through the four officer's files and those files had to be back in the HR office the next day or else there would be all sorts of mayhem breaking loose at the station. I decided that I should begin there but the information was just too much to go through in one night so I went out and bought a copier, something that would be able to carry the intended work load and could replicate originals without really showing too much that they had been copied. Between the four of them there were two hundred and fifty pages in their personnel files and each page containing crucial information that could be used at a later stage of my investigation.

The following day I prepared Selina things and put everything in the car and got ready for church. I didn't go all the way to our church instead I went to one of the local churches in the neighbourhood, I just wanted to be in the presence of God and to hear the gospel being preached and the same time ask God to help me in my venture because some of the things I had read in the files were terrifying but I was too far gone to turn back. If these people could ever find out that I was in their lives, they probably would kill me let alone imprison me and that was a gripping thought. The service lasted about an hour and the sermon was rather apt because it about Psalm 109, The complaint of a man in trouble. A man who asks God to save him from the persecutions of his fellowman and to grant him justice for the wrongs that they have done against him. His cries for help were so close to my own that I wept when I thought how much I had been a loyal and honest worker but got rewarded with scorn and hostility that I wept as I heard that pastor deliver his sermon with gusto and asking some probing questions. He asked if it was a case of being bullied or was the complaint a result of the goodness of the complainant being taken advantage of and again if the complainant was justified in asking God for such harsh sentences for his tormentors and then finally he asked what would we do if we were in this man's shoes. The service was truly an inspiration and a guide because it confirmed that I was not the first person to suffer such a fate but with faith and divine intervention, things do get better. I had received a new coat of armour and I was even more determined to see this task through to the end and I also remembered that when things began to get a little cloudy, I should just make a call to God and ask Him for help.

That Sunday's traffic at the police station was a bit hectic creating a disorderly atmosphere to the charge office, so I slipped Selina in through the back, changed into her uniform and with her trolley reappeared at the charge office desk and signalled to one of the cops for the key and because it was the same shift from the previous day he recognised me and beckoned me to enter into their work area and get it for myself from the senior's desk. The senior officers were not at the desk so it gave me a moment to scan their desk for any valuable information but there was nothing there so I took the key and one of the hand-held radios and a spare full battery from the charger on the floor alongside the desk. The route was a lot easier that time because it was first Tselane's office then the HR office to return the files and finally the IT office to fill up the two terabyte external hard drives. I lined up the tasks and files that were to be copied and left the computer to do its own thing while I carried on my charade of cleaning the police station and checking out what I could use. Four and half hours and a spotless police station later, I cleaned up the activity report and logged off the careless IT technician and clocked out and left. I returned to the station for the rest of the week and kept a watchful eye on my unsuspecting quarry, listening in on their phone calls and conversations with the colleagues picking up what their duties entailed and how they executed them. I also got to pick up my file from Molwedi's office, by right it should have been sent for storage but he was so backlogged, he had left it with the pile of other closed files on his floor. For a greater part none of the suspects acted out of character with the exception of Ndou and Ntumantuma who in one conversation, they referred to Le Roux and at first I thought the were talking about one of their colleagues but when they mentioned Yvonne and her email being connected again, it began to shed light on the ownership of Vuk'uzenzele: Senzile and Solile were their daughter and son which meant that they were the real beneficiaries of the contract. It was their palms that were being greased in the acquisition of the Vuk'uzenzele business.

I had sufficient information to tie these two up in fraud charges but I needed something more concrete in the event that they could evade those charges. I went into their files and checked the HR folders for their cell phone and land line itemised billing and started to see patterns and when I cross checked with their emails, I discovered the all important link between Ndou and Runze. Runze's commanding officer was Ndou's acquaintance and in an email, Ndou was scantily told about the bust on Phoenix Estate:

'...Phoenix was a friend, no initiating or follow up papers in place...just hold and shake for a while and keep on line for as long as possible...Your rank evaluation is in good hands, keep up the good work.

Commissioner JK Sphaka

Head of Crime Intelligence'

I was definitely getting in deeper than I had imagined but there was no way that I was going to back down, whoever this clown was he was first and foremost a human being and like I had seen from the files that I had collected locally, they all have personal lives which are just a mouse click or a photocopy away. On the Friday of that week, Selina went to work and bid her new friend Tselane goodbye because Rosina would be back at work on the following Monday but in actual fact Selina needed to solicit Director Ndou's assistance to get information from the national server and she had seen from cleaning his office that he has various programs but he used the same log in and password for all of them. I had already made a copy of his office key, so there wasn't a need to get into Tselane's office to get the hefty bunch and hung around for as long as was necessary waiting for all the admin staff to leave and to make sure that the big man himself was not coming back and for that I visited his car and disabled his tracking device using two cellphones which I retrieved from the evidence room. I attached the one phone to the inside of the grille, set it on silent and auto answer and thereafter I dialled it and the signals interfered with the tracking device. I checked his emails for further evidence and copied the emails he had sent to his private email address and from the national server, I called up information regarding Commissioner Sphaka, Superintendent Ntumantuma, Director Runze, Inspectors Swansea and Mabitla, Sergeants Moloi, Nuku, Chwe and Mokone and printed out all that I could access about them. As a final measure, I backed his system up on my hard drive and then crashed it with a couple of trojan and bugbear viruses that would keep on returning every time and because I didn't want to leave my fingerprints on his keyboard, I borrowed his secretary's one for the deed.

Commissioner Jasper Khulufelo Sphaka was born in 1954 in the village of Koringpunt, he matriculated in 1972 and immediately joined the police services in 1973. He significantly rose through the ranks from 1985 through to 1997 where he remained as a Captain in the Crime Intelligence Division and once again from 1999 through to 2007 he got promotions to Senior Superintendent and then finally made Divisional Commissioner in 2008. He has been a resident of Jozi since his Captaincy in 1991 and that was also the time when the country was almost in civil war but he made his name known from 1987 during the township riots. He was one of those cops that were known to patrol the townships rooting out guerrillas and suspected terrorists. He has been attributed to the break up and capture of many cells and received extensive training in urban tactical warfare. He got married to Sonto Mkhwanazi, who was a high school teacher, in 1985 and their first child Mildred Ntombi Mkhwanazi was born in 1982, their second child, Sophia Ratanang Sphaka, was born in 1986 and their son, Jasper Itumeleng Sphaka, was born in 1988. He received numerous commendations from his seniors and colleagues and on paper he had proven himself to be a top cop.

Superintendent Ntumantuma, was an academic cop. A township girl that became a policewoman and through the laws of Gender Equity, she was given the title. There was nothing about her career that made her stand out. She was born in the Kagiso in 1967, she matriculated at the age of twenty in 1987 and in 1992 she became a member of the bluemas police squad, a police force that comprised of the township SDU's (self defence units) which were essentially vigilantes that got a crash course in policing and were then given 12 gauge shotguns to patrol the streets. Most of these bluemasses were hoods and thugs that would have otherwise faced long prison terms if the real cops got to them, others were guerrilla wannabes and in Ntumantuma's case a groupie. She got married to an exile returnee and managed to go through labour thrice in 1994 and delivered Nkululeko Alisdair Ntumantuma, again in 1999 and gave unto the world Somandla Paul Ntumantuma and finally in 2004 she bore Thulisile Charity Ntumantuma.

Director Tinyiko Abednigo Runze was born in 1948 in Nsami

Dam village on the outskirts of Giyani in the then Northern Transvaal and in 1967 he received his highest education a JC (Junior Certificate), which was the equivalent of a Standard 8 (Grade 10). He was a through and through product of apartheid and wherever Verwoed lay he would be proud of that man. He revered the white man and probably almost fell apart when he was told that apartheid was over and that the new government was going to led by the Communists which he was trained to fight against. He started his law enforcement career as a mantshingilana (security) and then a mjanji (railway security) and then he joined the Suid Afrikaanse Polisie by the time he was twenty three. For a long time throughout his career, he remained a constable and an exceptional runner; he ran all sorts of errands for his white colleagues and superiors. He got transferred to Pietersburg (Polokwane) and got his promotion to Sergeant there in 1985. He has also been attributed to the capture of many dissidents in the Northern Transvaal area, especially when they were trying to make their escape out of the country through the Messina route. In 1991 he made detective and in 1994, as an Inspector, he was given an offer to transfer to Jozi. It took him another five years before he climbed the ladder and became a Captain where he remained as such until an in-house political blunder put him in line for Directorship in 2006. On the home front, he was a married man; twice in the sense that he had a customary wife back in Giyani and a civil wife in Jozi. He had a dozen children from both the marriages and the kids' birth dates ranged from 1975 through to 1998 all with staunch Xitsonga and biblical names.

Inspector Jacobus Swansea, was an ex soldier born in 1961 in the town of Paulpietersburg in Natal. He attended a catholic boarding school in the Ladysmith district and got accepted into the University of Natal but never attended because of financial constraints and national conscription laws of the time. He did his two years of army service and when he came back from the border in 1982, he joined the police. He was whisked through the ranks by virtue of his skin colour. He was married in 1985 but on the eve of their anniversary in 1996, a drunk driver left him widowed to raise their then four year old twins, Jacques and Jacqueline. His career highlights included stints in forensics for two years, narcotics for three years, three years in the riot squad, four years in the special branch and five years in the crime intelligence where he had received his promotion to Inspector. He had also been sent for rehabilitation twice in his career.

Inspector Markus Taunyana Mabitla was born 1950 in the old Germiston township of Dukathole. He matriculated in 1968 and furthered his education at the University of the North from 1970 to 1974 but due to family problems, he had to abandon that route and put the needs of the family ahead of his own. He got married in 1977 to Josephina Ntebohiseng Seenya and their children Sekgathaleng Esmeralda, Tiberius Anthony Mojalefa, Bontle Angelina and Bokamoso Francis were born in 1978, 1981, 1988 and 1990. He joined the force in 1975 as an administrator and in 1979 he joined the police academy. He made Detective in 1985 and received numerous commendations for bravery during the township uprisings of that era. He became a Major in 1995 but was demoted twice, first to Colonel in 2001 and then to Inspector 2006; both times for insubordination. He had been disciplined fourteen times, of which six of those disciplinary actions held were with him as a commissioned officer. He had also been taken for psychiatric evaluation for the more serious allegations that were brought against him, namely the unjustified shooting of an alleged suspect and fraudulent use of State resources for personal gains. His career was one filled with peaks and valleys of maladjusted behaviour.

Sergeant Isaac Lekguwa Moloi was a 1989 matriculant and a State ward born in 1971 in Attridgeville. He grew up in various foster homes and at the age of twenty-six, in 1997, he joined the police force to escape poverty and a life of crime which was knocking at his door. In 1995, he arrested for being in a stolen car but the charges against him were dropped after the investigation revealed that he was an unsuspecting accomplice in the joyride. He served his constabulary in Temba and got involved with a non governmental and a non profit organisations in the fight against drug abuse in the youth. Through the volunteer work that he had been involved in with those two organisations, his then Station Commander, put in a good word for him to join the Crime Intelligence Unit (CIU); the recommendation came through and he was made Sergeant in 2007. He was a single and had no recorded dependants.

Sergeant Zwelakhe Sizwe Nuku was born in 1969 in Dennilton. His highest recorded education was Standard 8 which he completed in 1985. Thereafter, he went underground when he joined one of the liberation movement's armed forces. In 1997, he was subpoenaed by the post apartheid truth commission to bear testimony of his involvement and activities in the armed struggle and he received amnesty for all his deeds. He changed careers from being a soldier to police officer in 2000 and because of his extensive experience, he was first placed in the VIP protection services but his sometimes volatile nature saw him being shunted around the various departments until he landed in the CIU in 2008 under the supervision of his old liberation army commanding officer who resigned from the service in 2009. This same supervisor's office had been in the same corridor as Tinyiko Runze for some time. He was not married but had seven dependants all listed as his children and all bearing different surname; two of his off spring were born in 1986 and three were born in 1998 and the last two were born in 2004 and 2005.

Sergeant Mpumelelo Chwe was a native of the Eastern Transvaal town of Ermelo was born 1970 and at the age of twenty-two years, he applied to join the police force but he was turned down for that 1992 in take. He applied again and again until he was accepted into the police academy in 1997. He graduated top of his class and showed promise to achieve great heights in his career as a police officer. There were no disciplinary actions in his file and his move to CIU was through recommendations and a proven track record; he was an exemplary cop in many aspects. He was single, had no children and listed his parents as his dependants.

Sergeant Tau Marcus Mokone born 1945 in Daveyton was another old guard of the old regiment. He joined the force in 1979 and kept pretty much to himself. He never exerted himself to stand out for his contribution in the various operations in which he was involved. He was a real deckhand of the police force and got to be Sergeant as a result of maturity rather than diligence. He was married to Tshifiwo Virginia Ndzundza in 1983 and they had six children: Mikateko Goodness born in 1985, Reuben Monnahadi born in 1987, Jonas Tautuna born in 1989, Stephina Maseemo born in 1993, Jocobeth Tshilidzi born in 1996 and Tryphina Letellang born in 2001.

I had the key figures in my investigation and all that remained to do was to observe them in their habitats and see who would be the most vulnerable and who would be the last to stand. The hard drive was loaded with information that would keep me busy for months on end whilst I planned the next phase of my own rendition of justice. In addition to their personnel files, I had some of the cases these cops had worked on and from there I would be able to see their diligence, weaknesses and modus operandi. With the exception of Chwe, the rest were quite sloppy in their work and quite often left loopholes in their work. Their statements were rushed or incomplete and suspects were not followed up with properly; their cases were mostly 'in a balance of probability' rather than 'beyond reasonable doubt' but oddly enough they were able to get a fair amount convictions, however if they had put in more elbow grease to their work, they would all have had eighty to ninety percent convictions. They had become complacent in the discharge of their duties, they were also of the belief that they were above reproach.

Since his appointment as the Commissioner, Sphaka had had a streak of indecisiveness and some of his decisions seemed dubious because he often gave the go ahead for raids on cases that were not fully investigated and that was evident in the number of cases that returned from the courts for further investigation. He had become a paper pusher wanting to please his superiors, where his great commendations came from and at the same time he wanted to gain popularity amongst his subordinates by giving them the feeling that he was the guy in charge and would always be there to back them up. On paper, he definitely was a great cop because there was an endless stream of papers coming from and going to his division but in reality he was a cop with political aspirations, a man who had lost the edge of being a tough street cop. He was a charismatic person but definitely not a fearless leader and he seemed to owe too many people, outside the service, favours and it was one of these favours that led to the paperless authorisation of an illegal search on my property that led to my unlawful and wrongful arrest.

It became clear that the rest of that crew just followed orders without question, as was expected in the police force and because the orders came from high up in the ranks, the matter got further sensationalised right through to the inconsistent media report and procedures.

THE PAUPER

After the verdict, Tobey went into a corner to lick his wounds, whilst I carried on trying to see that the false charges that were brought up against me were dropped and so there was no contact between us. We both were dealt further injustice by that judge and it was clear to see that Judas and Ashwiphe had invested in his legal skills but the greatest thing was having to prove it or wanting to prove it. It was highly likely that we never spoke any further because of the great disappointment and also because there were indications that Judas and Ashwipe wanted to sit down and settle things so that everyone would get a piece of the pie; a pie that I helped bake but would never get to have a taste of.

If those two parties were to get into bed together, I would have to be sacrificed; there would be no way that Ashwipe would want to deal with Tobey if I was still in the picture in any way or form and Tobey knew that that cash cow at the airport was just too fat to let go of on the basis of ethics and unwritten promises to me. I knew that and I was not willing to let myself or my family go thorough another ordeal lie the one that I had just experienced, so I chose to withdraw from the gang and case number 139/3/2010 was still looming over my head like an executioners axe and until that had been withdrawn, I did not want to cause any further ripples.

Tobey came from a poor white Afrikaner family and grew up in the apartheid era, he completed his matric and as was the order of the day, he was conscripted and he served his country like many of his fellow young and uninformed white friends and family. He was stationed in Angola and he defended his country's borders well, so well that he received a medal of honour and when he returned from the army he joined the police services and was told that there was a new threat that was encroaching, the threat of 'Black Power' where if it was left unchecked it would destabilise the entire lifeline of the Republic. Once again he heeded to the call to arms and as a police officer he became a Warrant Officer and made sure that the enemies of the State were duly out behind bars and punished for their heinous crimes. He met up with Alwyn during his years in the police force and their friendship has survived many a challenge and hardship. Alwyn didn't quite have the stomach for the apartheid propaganda so he left the service before Tobey and he studied law and became a lawyer and a damn good one at that. By the time Tobey realised that he had been lied to, it was too late to amend his deeds so he did what any smart white person facing multiple homicides, prison or poverty would do; he applied for amnesty and aligned himself with the upcoming regime of the 'Swart Gevaar' (Black Danger) and from there he learnt how to become a businessman, wheeling and dealing his way out of the abyss that was waiting for him. In truth, he merely sidestepped falling into the pit but his slate has not yet been wiped clean. He runs a clean ship but it is too late to cover up the blood and tears of all those that fell under his command and those he trampled upon to get to his millions.

His file from the list of dossiers that I had lifted, courtesy of Ndou, had more blackouts than Eskom's load shedding schedule of Jozi. Somebody purposely kept him blacked out in order to protect themselves or a clandestine group and I knew if I ventured too far into that avenue, I would end up swimming with the fish or wake up on board a slave vessel, somewhere in the Mediterranean Sea. What I saw in his records was enough to keep me at bay and I wondered if he was really going to be worth my while or should I leave him to the system because the system of the day had its own way of getting at the monsters that it had created; though some may have survived the initial cleansing but in the ultimate end they all got their day in court or in the morgue. If I had taken Tobey on, it would have meant having to take on a third of the government, if not more and that was not what this crusade was about; I wasn't looking for martyrdom or to start a revolution, I just simply wanted heart wrenching, spirit breaking revenge and Tobey's inclusion in that would have derailed my cause for a greater cause of humanity. In as much as I then felt that something should be done about all the corruption and deceit that some of our government and corporate leaders had engaged in, like many of my countrymen and women, I was not willing to get out of my comfort zone to take them head on. The truth of it all, I felt that that was not my fight, yet; mine was with Ashwipe and especially Judas, the country had its own issues and avenues to sort out their muck. I also knew that that type of thinking was not right but I consoled myself with the thought that what could one man do? They are after all the government and they could make things even more unbearable than what they already were and I did not want to risk that. So for the moment Tobey would be off limits and I had to settle for the other two guppies and their cronies and they were proving to be enough for my plate, as a matter of fact they were already giving me serious indigestion before I had even finished the course.

LE PETIT BOURGEOIS

I was only introduced to the tip of the iceberg; the man was a myriad of secrets and enigmas. Questions led to more questions and it was a frustrating time trying to resolve the mystery behind the man. I realised that with Ashwipe I had been placing too much emphasis on what I could lay my hands on rather than what he would or had willingly given me. I followed paper trails that led nowhere, unfounded and uncollaborated accusations and even court documents that I could get hold of were not as strong as what I had hoped for. His credit cards and other financial statements were as vague as a he was but somehow he had amassed all the wealth he had and with what I had heard from him and seen of him, no such amount of money could be all clean. I tracked back to the things that he had said, the places that he had visited, the people that he had worked for and with, the people that he had grown up with and especially the people that he had pissed off but there wasn't enough for me to hurt him the way I wanted to, even if I pieced together all that I had on him, at best it would just shock him but not incriminate him in anything. He reminded me of a riddle that I was once asked when I was a teenager and this riddle had me in thought for a long time: 'A man is discovered dead, hanging from the rafter in a room that only has a door and no windows. There is no chair, steps or anything that he could have stood on. On the floor there is a puddle of water. How did he manage to hang himself?'

The answer to that was not as complex as I had thought it would be but because of the way I had been trained and brought up to think, I kept on looking past the answer. Every answer that I had suggested was from something that I brought into the room and not what was in there already, nothing in there seemed plausible to have assisted the dead man to end his own life. It didn't, or rather; I didn't want to believe that a person could do such a thing to their person. It always seemed to me that the laws of self-preservation would kick in and stop the act and then I would then think about how intense his problems would have been for him to commit suicide and that would then veer me off the riddle and then I would shelf it for as I continued to ponder the aspects of problems in one's life, trauma to the family, the religious aspects of suicide - would he be allowed into heaven or would God forgive him for his sins? The riddle remained unanswered yet I would get as many questions as I got answers to life in general. One of the answers that I got in the debates that followed that riddle was that as people we are creatures of habit and we tend to repeat things, especially if those things or habits benefit us, even if they could be harmful or hurtful to others, we would repeat those deeds; an example of that would be the criminal. A criminal often claims that their actions were spurned by circumstance but at the core of it all they know that their actions are illegal and tend to cause harm to others and then the justice system highlights to them that because there are benefits, financial or otherwise, to the criminal they did not stop to think about the adverse consequences that those actions would have on the other party and unless they had been caught they would have continued with their unacceptable behaviour so it then remains the duty of the criminal justice system to force them to stop or inspire them to change their habits.

Ashwiphe had a very loose family link; he was not as bonded to his family as was Judas was to his. He was far more advantaged, he was an international child star with a promising movie career but he was not lazy or believed that it was just dropped into his lap; he did his fair share of work. He was well spoken and raised with some degree of morals and values; the value that was greatly punted in him was that the winner takes all and do all it takes to win. Understandably, considering that he had to compete with many other child performers from around the world to land the roles that he got, so he could not afford to be lax in going for the auditions. Even though he was only about eight years old when he began his career, he was coached and coaxed to be vigilant in securing those roles. He was an adorable performer on the screen but the side effects of all of that were that the all or nothing approach was left deeply entrenched in his being and there could be not turning it off. On the home front, he followed the same regime and it soon became unbearable for his parents and so they shipped him off to boarding school where, hopefully, the influence of the other kids would help him readjust to being a normal child. Unfortunately, things didn't go according to plan because in boarding school, he was bullied and taunted and institutionalized and when he finally retaliated, the initial mentality and values of win at all cost and do whatever it takes to survive kicked in and got cemented into his being. He began hustling and really got into the boarding school self-rule vibe; he had to depend on himself in order to defend himself, there were no set security or parents nearby to bail him out. He had only himself to rely on, he felt that his family had abandoned him and as each year went on and he had to return to that dreaded school, he loathed his family even more. When he left school, he found any reason not to return home because at home they had rules that he would have to abide by and those were not the rules that he had been accustomed to, as a matter of fact he felt that he owed those people nothing; if anything, they had to pay him for the grief they had caused him by shipping him off to that academic prison but in some way he was also glad that they sent him there because he had learnt so much about the world and its cruelty and he was especially proud of the fact that he had acquired the skills to beat any system.

He continued hustling and getting by and saving each dime he hustled. He often reverted back to his safe haven: the movie industry to try out for another block buster but he just kept on bumming out. He had hoped that with a big break in that world, which had a great sense of familiarity and safety, he would show all those kids that used to make fun of him at school that he was not a has been and that he still had a sparkle in his star. The movie world would also have served as an escape from the harshness of the real world because in character he could be in a world that suited him. He never really got back to his former glory of being an international star, the best and the highest that he could attain in front of a camera was to be a presenter on a Bantustan television station and with the democratisation of the country both homeland and television station were integrated into the land but unfortunately his program got the axe. The new executives felt that it wasn't just the right time to expose the nation to that type of content; they said people were more interested in the upcoming truth hearings and not some airy-fairy snot nosed teenager program about being born at the right time; he was crushed but he kept his chin up and didn't give up that easily. He tried his hand at producing and directing but that also had limited success, as a matter of fact he completely bombed out as a director and the critics were quite undecorated with their critiques and it was that harshness of their views that saw him backing away from the industry, licking his wounds. He was soon back onto hustling and scheming and in an episode of his delusions of grandeur, he saw himself as a media mogul. It was a great plan which had subtle hints of Hitlerism in it, in that he wanted to be the most powerful media executive and take down all those who had opposed him or stood in his way and especially those that belittled him. His embarkation upon that journey made him realise that in order to make it to the top of that ladder he had to have a lot of muscle and backing so he began prostituting his skills politically. His presumption, along with many other misguided souls, was that as a party member, friend or ally of ruling party, he would have better access and to certain jobs and as a relative of an exile he would get preferential treatment. According to him, he was aligning himself with the eagles and thus he was set for success but all that was basically asserting the fact that there was no more talent, no more realistic dreams and the avenues for hustling were leading into dark dingy alleys and though he was right at home there, he wanted to upscale his deals. One shady deal after another he continued to amass his wealth but with little or no paper trail. The businesses that he had registered were doing ok but not substantial enough to sustain the lifestyle he was living and if he was pushed into a corner, he made it seem that his wealth was old money and he was still a struggling entrepreneur.

That was his modus operandi! He was moving the money through his estranged family or a third party; all he was receiving was commissions, grants, gifts and awards: no salaries as most of his transactions were cash based. Just like the riddle of the man in the room, the answer was the liquid under his feet. He stood on a block of ice and it slowly melted until he asphyxiated; truly a cruel way to self-terminate but each to their own I suppose. Ashwiphe's solution would be that; to simply isolate him off from his funds, which meant taking away his credibility with his backers and friends. I would be just mirroring him the favour that he did for me when he and Judas sent their lackey over to visit me and plant their Phenacetin in my house. It wasn't about sending me to jail but more about discrediting me in the eyes of the law. He knew that if they could show the magistrate that I was in some way involved in illegal activities then it was likely that Tobey's civil suit would fall apart. It was a pity that that magistrate did have enough neurological activity to figure that out, especially when they presented him with a criminal case from 1989 and again with another where the alleged suspect was arrested on the same day that the responding affidavits were submitted but I suppose then he wasn't in the class when the lecturer covered the topic of reasonable doubt and witness credibility.

Ashwiphe's downfall would be his social standing, work and money and I had just the right virus for that. He almost always had his meetings at an up market strip joint and I would get a part time job there as a deckhand which would be even allow me to get close enough to him without him getting too suspicious. He wasn't much of a drinker, so spiking his drink would not really work and he really didn't part-take in the saucy activities that were on offer at the premises, so getting one of the ladies to do a number on him would also be out of the question. He was friends with the owner which made things even trickier in that he had some protection from the security; just the type of lifestyle that he wanted and he was friendly enough with most of the staff but just enough to have them on his side and for them to think highly of him. The plan was for me to wait for a night when he had had two or three drinks and I would let out the air from his tyre and his spare, which was under his car and then I would followed him, he would have to eventually stop to explore the thump-thumping noise of the flat and I would hung back for a few minutes while he made a couple of calls as he was trying to access his spare. As he pulled it out and discovered that it was also flat, I would drive up to him and offer to help him and being out in the dimly lit roadside, I wasn't even worried that he would identify me and so I would begin changing his tyre and then offer to go pump his spare for him at the nearest garage, knowing him to be the egotistical, materialistic person that he was, he would never agree to leave his car unattended, so I would offer to leave my bag with him so that he would see that I would return to collect my possessions. In his desperation he would agree to my terms and I would take off with his tyre. On my way to the garage, I would stop off at a payphone and anonymously called the police and advise them as a concerned citizen that there was a suspicious black Cheyenne on the road which had been driving about recklessly for a couple of kilometres. After the call I would drive around the block and backtrack with the tyre on foot and dump it within a hundred metres of his car. The dumped tyre would be a replica that would be inflated with an adequate amount of white powder which would be a concoction of bicarbonate of soda, aspirin, paracetamol and codeine. The powder mass would be dense enough to convince any blundering cop that it was narcotics. The cops would find him at the spot that I would have directed them to and a search would revealed a bag that would have a tightly bound brick of white powder which had would sprinkled with just enough phenacetin so that when they did a test it would be enough to convince them that they have the real deal but once it went to the forensics lab it would be a dud.

I would park across the road and video the search and arrest with a night vision camera and the look on his face as the cops make the discovery would be absolutely worth every waking moment of planning.

THE PEDAGOGUE

'Bless me father for I have sinned, it has been too long for me to remember since my last confession. Father, I have strayed so far from the path of righteousness that I do not even know what it means to be righteous. My virtues have been so tainted that I only consider them to be vices. I used to think that doing the right thing would help me and guide me on a path of morality but now I am not sure. I have judged, I cannot forgive and I am filled with hatred. As each day passes, I find myself slipping towards a dark and sombre side and this veering off seems to grow more and more. As someone who was raised in the sanctuary of your house, I have always been more partial towards those that serve You and have held dear their teachings but now I doubt the truth that I have been weaned on.'

The church, what a wonderfully sanctimonious place. A place where we are destined to find serenity, inner peace and a better understanding of ourselves, especially our spirituality. A place where we are given the opportunity to connect with Our Creator and His Divine unconditional love, where we get the chance to revive our relationship with Him through the message that gets delivered to us by His anointed and self appointed servants. The men and women whom He called and gave the choice to follow in Aaron's and Peter's shoes and such a noble and yet humbling opportunity it is. Is man the right instrument to teach righteousness and guide us on the moral code where he, himself is susceptible to the same temptations that he teaches us to steer clear from?

From early childhood, just like the police and other uniformed people, we are taught to revere the clergy; they are presented to us as representatives of God on earth and somewhere in the recesses of our brains we translate that to the fact that, they are therefore infallible and could do no wrong. I suppose it's a longing in us to constantly see holiness whilst we are in this life or possibly to see that faith works and that it's more than just an intangible feeling or notion. When I heard of all the marvellous things that the late Archbishop Masango had done, how he had helped so many people through prayer, it kept my faith alive and it spurned me on to keep on praying and believing. His ministry helped me believe that through prayer and by being close to the house of God, things could never go horribly wrong. At first, in my naivety as a child, I thought that people believed in him and thought of him as God but with age and having heard some of his sermons (some being testimonials by my parents and other family friends), I realised that they believed in the fact that if they took their problems to him and prayed earnestly with him then God would hear their prayers a lot sooner or a lot clearer. Just like it was with Moses and the children of Israel, he was a channel for their belief and not the answer to their prayers and just as the Israelites used to refer to Jehovah as Moses' God, the children of St. John's Apostolic Faith Mission often used the phrase 'Molimo oa Ntate Masango...' ('The God of Father Masango...') and even in the 21st century, a lot of the old congregation that prayed with him still used that phrase in their prayers, almost thirty years after he had passed on. To a multitude, he was the epitome of holiness and people were happy to believe that what he believed in was correct and that it worked. They tithed with conviction and again with the belief that it was for the good of the church as laid down in the scriptures.

When he passed on however, things changed and for the worst because there were power plays, political and personal financial agendas. Some factions wanted a spiritual leader who would be able to carry on with the work that had been started, others wanted a leader that would just be a figure head for the church and others just wanted to be in power for the sake of power and respect. He never left a 'will' as to who should take over the church because he never saw the church as his own personal empire but he did leave a will as to what should become of his businesses: he gave them to his two grandsons. He knew the difference between personal and clerical: the church was never his to own and thus hand over; the church had to elect its own leader. After fifteen years of endless squabbling and bickering and the realisation of his prophecies, St. John's finally got a new Archbishop which was elected through ballot and some legal intervention and the prophecy that the church would split again came true. The church split into groups that were loyal to him and his teachings, groups that were loyal to his predecessor, The Lady Archbishop Nku and the group that saw the church as a money making scheme.

One such person that saw opportunity in these splits was a business man by the name of Joseph Moripe. He managed to convince the new Archbishop to ordain him as a priest and then used his power to get into the church coffers and from his resources, his business acumen and street smarts, he garnered enough strength through the weaknesses created by the endless backbiting and built an alliance within the church that helped him to create a sizeable nest egg to retire on. This man really went to town on his expenditures, he bought farms, refinanced his businesses, bought land and built the Archbishop a majestic mansion on that land, which he then told the congregation it was the Archbishop's retreat, which was extremely odd though because that retreat was built in the suburbs and the Archbishop's old house in the township had received a makeover. The Archbishop himself was content to sit in his newly built office and count money and fret over financial matters instead of ministering to people and when he got into church for service, it was farcical because he attempted so much to sound like the Late Archbishop Masango, from the intonation of his voice right through to hand gestures. However, when he realised that all that still did not get him the full respect of all the old guard clergy, Moripe convinced him that he needed to get an honourary doctorate from an academic institution and then he would be a bigger and better leader than his predecessor, well as far as the learned community was concerned. After some shady deals were done, the church band - the once prophesised soldiers of the faith, were packed into three busses and herded to some lecture hall in the East Coast. In a jubilant ceremony, a Doctorate of Divinity was bestowed upon the Archbishop and some popular gospel singer but even that did not get him the respect of the elder clergy or the learned community, as Moripe had promised, so the next plot was to get him a cappa magna and mitre that was to show him as a greater prophet and leader than Archbishop Masango. It was shortly after he got the crimson cappa magna that the Archbishop's health began to fail him and within two years of that robing, he passed on at a mental institute. His wife and Moripe then began a daring move to change the constitution of the church and in that they wanted to include a clause which allowed for the authority of the church to shift from the husband to the wife. This would have meant that any and all circuits would then be given to the family's that were deployed to run them, thus making the churches family possessions but most importantly it would have meant that she would have had full ownership of the headquarters and she would have transferred ownership to her children when she passed on. In a twist of events, Moripe moved into the Archbishop's 'retreat' with the widow Lady Archbishop and cleaved himself from his wife and children. He also took possession of the luxury German cars that were bought for the Archbishop, which were purchased at his insistence and pleading with the congregation that the Archbishop needed such extravagance for his image and travels and the saddest part was that the congregation tithed and collected money so that those sedans would be acquired. The choice of brand was also not just coincidental because the Late Archbishop and Lady Archbishop Masango were also chauffeured around with Merc's but the difference was that theirs were financed through their shops; the shops which they left to their grandsons.

A group of older bishops had had enough of this opulence and decided that according to the standing constitution, which was still legal and binding were going to elect a new leader and in an off site general meeting, because anyone who did not want to say 'Molimo oa Ntate Maroga...' (God of Father Maroga...) was deemed to be a heathen and thus excommunicated from the church. There was just something about the two names: Masango is an Nguni word for gates and Maroga is a Sotho word for curses and I suppose that that in it could be a reason why a lot of the congregation was not too keen to refer to his God but happily did so with his predecessor. Once the decision had been made in the conference and the voting was done, the newly appointed Archbishop was going to be presented to the congregation at the headquarters.

On the afternoon of 04 June 2005, Archbishop Sebenza and the old guard from Archbishop Masango headed to Katlehong and as soon as they had entered the gates of the church yard and no sooner had they alighted their cars, they were descended upon by hired impis from the hostel and Kwa-Zulu Natal. They pounced on the unsuspecting and defenceless old men and pummelled them. They beat them with sticks, knob-kierries, short spears and any weapon that they lay their hands on. My father had been part of the convoy and sadly he received his fair share of the ambush on holy ground. The swarm of mercenaries were merciless in their exection of their tasks and they made sure that everyone that was in that convoy was treated fairly, according to their job specs. They beat the old men and women into submission and if it had not been for a group of local residents passing by that recognised my father's, there would have been fatalities on that day. The locals raised an alarm and started charging at the impis with stones and within moments other members of the community were out of their houses and had joined the cavalry. The impis' attack was repelled and the convoy was then able to get out of the church yard and into the safety of the community. The cowardly Moripe, who had been spotted standing at a distance earlier during the attack, slipped away like a snake shedding its skin, using one of the church's side entrances. Another person who had also taken flight during the attacks was a young man by the name of Sintle Qhalile. Sintle had been at the core of the appointment of Archbishop Sebenza, he had been rallying support for a new leader and had made it his mission to make sure that all of the old guard bishops were pulling together to elect a new church leader in accordance with the constitution. He doled out cash from his own pocket to ensure the legitimacy of the constitution and that even if it was challenged in a court of law that the opposition would have very little grounds for a lengthy drawn out legal battle. His heart was definitely in the right place and he really did mean well but he was ill prepared for the outcome of that fateful day. Prior to that day he gave assurances that he would have a strong security detail to protect the old men when they entered the church grounds and that the security would be none other than the elite Scorpions but none of that materialised as my father, the newly elected Archbishop Sebenza, Bishop and Lady Bishop Boniswa from the West Rand diocese, Bishop and Lady Bishop Tumiso from the Free State diocese and eleven others were stabbed and wounded and would have been dead if it were not for the good Samaritans that were passing along. That was the last that anyone heard of young crusader Sintle Qhalile, he, his well meaning intentions and his newly started foundation fizzled into the very thin air that it had manifested from.

'Mat! Hello,' I casually answered the phone.

'Junior, uBaba use sibhedlela...' (Junior, dad's in hospital)

'Sis Sarah!?! Kuwenze njani?!? Siph' isbhedlela?!?' (Sarah? What happened? Which hospital?).

'Lalela. Uzoba right, akalimalanga ka khulu. Babashayile lapha esontweni kodwa akekho o shonile babalimazile, manje amambulansi thwele okubamukisa e Natalspruit.' (Listen. He's going to be alright, he's not severely injured. They were beaten up at church and there were no fatalities, it's just that they were injured and right now the ambulances have taken them to Natalspruit hospital), Sarah said trying to keep the news as a-matter-of-factly as possible.

'Uph' umama? Is she alright?' (Where's mom?) I asked expect-ing to hear more woes,

'Nangu lapha. She's gathering her things and we're going to the hospital to meet up with Seipati' (She's here...) and as my sis-ter spoke, I could hear my mother's voice in the background, sounding every bit as motherly and wifely as possible; taking charge and giving orders to every to stay calm and not to let anyone in the house once they had left and that's when my mind shut off.

I was at home with Giovanni and we'd been doing some cook-ing and playstation and had a couple of movies that we were going to settle into for the evening when I got that alarming call. I bellowed for Vanni to get his go bag, which was always packed and ready for any trip we could have fancied taking. We were after all, bachelors. Technically, he was a junior bachelor and I had just been re-bachelorised or in the process thereof as the divorce hadn't been fully settled but all the same we were bachelors. His younger siblings Mpho and Neo were staying with their mom, my ex-wife in the making, as part of the di-vorce settlement and I would only pick them up every second weekend. I was trying to adjust to the new life of being a di-vorce. I was in the midst of reflecting on how I had exacerbated things, how had I pushed her away and what direction was I going to take after the pain had subsided? The pain! There are no words that could fully describe the pain associated with divorce but I can say that it definitely is not an affliction that I would wish upon my worst enemy. Divorce, strips away civil-ity and that's after it has made sure that there is no more space for the love to return and try to make some effort of reconciliation. In divorce, we see the worst of the people we once loved; they are no longer the cutie hotties that we were so gaga about they become transformed into hideous, monstrous, selfish, thoughtless trollops or abusive bastards as reason gives way to unchecked and unjustifiable emotion. She accused me of being abusive, verbally, psychologically and physically and I retaliated with that she was a lazy and an unfit mother, always denying me of sexual pleasure and the insults and provocations never ceased but then again those were the causes of the divorce and not the divorce in itself. Sure enough when I sat back and recalled some of my actions, I realised that I could have handled things a lot differently and the outcome would probably have been more amicable. However, I would also recall that I took that approach when she had walked out of our marriage the first time and we ended up being separated for eight months and I finally decided to sit down with her and try again.

Now all those incidents were things that were occupying my mind on the days, weeks and months that followed and the day my father got attacked was not too different; the only exception was that I had not begun drinking as it had become customary for me to down a bottle of bourbon whiskey or vodka and six pack of ciders and at times I didn't even care what brand it was, just as long as it would numb the senses and render me unconscious, sometimes in the hopes that I would get alcohol poisoning and the pain would stop permanently. I shepherded Vanni into the car and instructed him to buckle up and keep his eyes on the road; I didn't want him to see the modest arms cache that I had packed into the backseat. It consisted of a Winchester 12 gauge pump action and a 9mm Uzzi along with close to one thousand rounds of ammunition and on me I had a 9mm short Browning double action pistol on the left ankle, a .38 snub nosed revolver on the right ankle, a 9mm Glock 19 on the left hip, a 9mm CZ in the shoulder holster and some extra clips in my favourite leather jacket, which my father had bought for me on one of his business trips in Chile. I wasn't going to war; I was going to a massacre and execution. The people who were responsible for putting my father in hospital were not going to see the light of day; I was going to leave a trail of blood, guts and bodies in my wake. If history had taught people that the Vikings and all the other conquerors of the old world were savage then I was about to rewrite history as we knew it. I headed onto the freeway and within moments I was doing 180km/h and still accelerating. The car held fast onto the ground, it was an Audi A4, 2.0 and I knew how to get the most out of it and as we hit the 220km/h mark, Vanni pipped:

'Daddy's very angry, isn't he? Somebody's messed with daddy's family neh?'

He perched himself up to get a view of the world as it whizzed by. I heard him but didn't want to answer him because then I would have to come back to my senses and realise that I was about to unleash a Leviathan onto that church and its self appointed leader, Joseph Moripe. In my mental acknowledgement of Vanni's question, I eased my foot off the accelerator and hugged the Bucchleuch interchange curve and joined the N3 Durban and as soon as I the front tyres met up with the N3, an oncoming car began picking up speed and as its headlights drew nearer to Nkoboli GP, I dropped to four and let her take a breath of fresh air and let her have her own way with the road. She flared her and mockingly asked me if that's all I had and I dropped my lead laden foot on her and she squealed as I let her climb back to the 200's and when she hit 215km/h I let her rest at fifth gear and pressed my foot in until it felt like it was boring a hole through into the engine and she let rip. The car that was almost a threat became a dim light and I focused on the approaching red lights in front. We bobbed and weaved through the Saturday night revellers and night traffic and within moments we were passing Edenvale and approaching Giloolly's Interchange. I didn't even think about the possible police presence there or the endless accidents that always occur there, I just looked three cars in front of me and kept pushing and within seconds we were gliding past Van Buuren Road off ramp and I knew that from there it was going to be smooth sailing as most of the traffic would have turned off there or at the M2 West. My fastest time between Midrand and Katlehong had been twenty-seven minutes but on 04 June 2005, I did that trip in 18 minutes. 18 minutes is all it took me to park that road devastator outside Sarah's house. Vanni unbuckled and I took him inside the house, checked if my nephews and niece were alright and then took two empty twenty-five litre drums and headed for Natalspruit hospital which was only five minutes away. The security guards at the gates did their mundane duty and allowed me in and after parking the furious car, I headed for the casualty ward. I was met by Steward, Seipati's husband, at the door and he ushered me outside and ordered me to stand down. It was apparent that they had been told that I was packing a lot of heat and they knew what that meant. He was shortly joined by Marks and then Sarah and Seipati and they ordered, begged and pleaded with me to calm down as dad was not seriously injured, by that they meant that he wasn't on a stretcher with his bowels hanging out and that he was very much conscious and being his usual self. I tried to break through the gathering and as I did, mom appeared behind them. She had just joined the group but because of her diminutive stature and my heightened emotional level I didn't see her and soon as I heard her voice, the beast that had been roused earlier on, retreated slowly at first and then went back to its cage. She took me by the hand back to the car and told me to disarm. I was reluctant but at the same time so powerless that I took every piece of remorseless metal of me, even the steak knives which I had tucked into the jacket. All she had said was that if I wanted to see my father then I had to be his child and not the beast that I had dragged out of its abyss.

Natalspruit hospital! A shabby and almost run down state

medical facility that was infamous for its mortality more than anything else. From the clerks who thought that they were a cut above the rest to the nurses who thought that they crapped ice cream to the doctors who were never there when needed. The place was a pit and I recalled the summer 1980 when Seipati and I were involved in car accident just outside Katlehong and we had to be taken to Natalspruit hospital to receive emergency attention. Firstly, it took almost an hour for an ambulance to come from the hospital which was only seven kilometres away from the accident scene and then Seipati only got attended to at about 01h00 after having been there from about 16h00 and if it wasn't for my father's belligerence and threats to call the health superintendent and the media, my sister would have surely have died from her injuries in the corridors of that place. Some of the nurses were making snide remarks, asking who did my father think he is by making such threats and carrying on like a raving lunatic and now on that day the roles were reversed, Seipati and I were the ones threatening to call in the big brass and fortunately there was a family friend, who had been renting one of our properties, that had just come on duty and he immediately attended to my father and the other clergymen and their spouses. Dad had been beaten on the temple and back with an iron rod and stabbed in the chest, just above the heart and wrist with a makeshift spear but those wounds were superficial and only required a couple of stitches. We were only going to find out the extent of the internal injuries when it became evident that dad would need a number of eye operations and a back operation which he received over the following three years but even with that, he has never fully recovered from those injuries.

A criminal case was opened against Moripe and his four henchmen even with the overwhelming medical evidence and doctor's testimony, he was found not guilty and the charges against him were dropped and when dad decided to take his lawyers on for their flagrant display of unethical behaviour, he was once again done in by the Justice system and I hated myself for not having dispensed justice then.

Dad heard of what I had intended to do and though he found it noble he sat me down and talked some sense into me. He showed me his view points and pointed out that though he would have done exactly the same thing and how his teachings of revenge and vengeance had been wrong. He placed emphasis on '...forgive us our trespasses, as we forgive those who trespass against us...' and most importantly he said that he didn't want to lose me to some dark force that he was almost sucked wholly into.

'Junior, you mean the world to me and I would never be able to go on if you were to die or go to prison because of what happened to me. That, son; is my fight. God knows what he is doing and I sure know that there are some of my own sins that I have to pay for, so please don't make it more difficult for me to bear by having me watch you slip away from my life. Your presence in my life helps me make sense of whatever clutter there is in it. I know it's difficult but please do it for me. When I taught you how to handle and shoot a firearm, I told you that a gun was not for revenge but for self defence and if you had gone through with your plan; you would have been a cold blooded killer and not the man I had worked hard to raise. You're a excellent son, an amazing father and you were a great husband and I am proud of what you have achieved in your life, so don't throw it away on a whim and please stop drinking because there will be no solution in that bottle just more misery and woes.'

What? Stop drinking? How do he even know that I was still drinking, I mean I did everything possible to keep it away from him. Besides part of the reason that I was drinking was to subdue the horrible beast that was inside, that demon that lurked in every one of my dreams; the one that made wake up every night in cold sweats and shortness of breath. Every night I had a similar dream, I would be walking in a dark street or environment and I could hear rustling, panting and growling in the darkness and when I least expect it, a beast or a band of marauders would suddenly appear in front of me or surround me and they would lunge at me mercilessly until my body was numb and even if I were to open my eyes it would feel like they were still pulling and tearing at me. At times I would be able to run towards the lantern or lamp post where they would just evaporate and I could then wake up gasping for air but just as tired as if I had been in a boxing match or a marathon. I had become afraid of sleep but I couldn't do without it and it didn't matter if I dozed off during the day or went into a deep slumber at night; the nightmares were there and at the centre of them all was the beast which seemed to be championing this cause and taunting me to do battle with it, knowing full well that I would lose and once I had lost then I would belong to it and it's forces. Sometimes I just wanted to give into it and let it have its way with me but something or specifically someone would pull me back and tell me to hold on as I felt myself lose consciousness. Often I would go to bed completely soused, not even remembering how I drove home but as soon as the dreams began then I would be sober and I would remember everything from the first drink right through to the moment before I woke up drenched in sweat and if I woke up in a dark room, I would still feel the beast receding back into one of the corners of the bedroom and its stench still lingering in the bedroom. With that I would reach for a bottle of Bourbon or whatever was available that was stored behind the bed or in the nightstand and I would slug it down like I was drinking water from the tap. I could neither smell its fumes nor feel it burning my internal organs as it made it fiery way down into my stomach and shortly after that I would pass out again but only to repeat the process again in an hour or two until daybreak. Now my father wanted me to stop, what could he offer me to quell those nightmares? Nothing, that's what.

I knew that what he saying was true, after all he had never told me anything that didn't make sense but I wasn't ready to let go of my liquor and this route of forgiveness that he had asked to take was quite a lot to chew in itself. I had to forgive Moripe and at the same time I had been toying with forgiving my ex wife and again that was a big deal.

THE WORD

Judas Dlova was also a man of the cloth and I suppose that was what drew me closer to him; I felt that with all that had happened to me at KZN, Expressed and the Airways, he would be much easier to work with and get along with. I had worked with him in the Airways and I knew him to be a hard task master but I didn't mind that at all because the results were absolutely incredible and gratifying to say the least; he was able to bring out the best and sometimes the worst in a person.

He was born and raised in the South West Rand and had lost both his parents but he didn't grow up to be a bitter man, as a matter of fact he was quite a jolly fella possibly because he had the gift of the Holy Spirit; he was a clairvoyant or maybe he was just good at praying and dealing with adversity. From early childhood, unlike some of us, he embraced his disposition and saw it as a gift rather than a curse. He had a few friends, more correctly acquaintances and colleagues but no one that he could call a best friend in every common sense of the word and he was alright with that; he had made his peace that he was a different from the other kids. This acceptance further counted in his favour because he became focused and could allot all his time to his studies or to work or whatever project that he had embarked upon and he made the best of his situation and made every situation count. When he was ten years old, his father passed on due to illness and he his four sisters were rasied by his mother and grandmother. Grandma Dlova was especially fond of her grandson and did all in her power to cocoon him from the harshness and cruelty of the world. She took him to every church service and conference that she went to and to all her society gatherings. Her motives though were not as pure as they seemed in that, her helping to raise little Judas was not just about relieving her daughter-in-law from the stresses of raising five children alone. Not at all; in a way, she wanted to complete the task of raising her own late son and she saw and seized the opportunity in doing it through her grandson. She was intent on ensuring that her, the Dlova, family values, traditions and customs would survive because her own children had failed to do so. The one son, Klaas, was a jailbird and the other, Calvin, well let's just say he loved women; excessively. As for her daughters, Nokuzuko was a complete trollop, Daphne had eloped and Gloria had left to study in the Cape Province but that was well before Judas was born and she had not returned since. There were rumours and strange stories, as there usually were in such neighbourhoods, about Grandma Dlova; stories that she had conceived twelve times and the six that remained were the ones that had survived her sacrificial rituals to her deity because she was believed to have been a member of an occult. Those that had grown up with her and knew her from the rural Natal village of oSizweni, situated about twenty kilometres east of Newcastle, said she always stood out amongst the girls. She was said to be very intimidating and with just a single look, she could reduce a person to a whimsical existence in her presence; Grandma Dlova, born Ntombikayise Precious Nkosi, was a woman who had a different and somewhat difficult childhood because of what she was born with; the ability to see glimpses of the future.

When Ntombi was still a young maiden in the village of oSizweni, some of the girls in the village would tease and taunt her, saying that uthakathiwe (bewitch) because without warning she would rant in an incoherent gibberish or by just touching another person, she would tell them of imminent danger. She once told one of the girls that her mother would punish her severely for breaking ukhamba (clay pot) that the girl's mother had received as part of her bridal gifts from her mother when she got married. When it happened, just as Ntombi had predicted, the girls who were there when Ntombi foretold the incident told their mothers and as the news went from house to house it got more than its fair share of embellishment until the facts were so distorted that the newsworthy version that was making the rounds said that Ntombi had bewitched the other young girl because she was envious of that girl and her family's good fortunes. The girl's family having heard the sensationalist version consulted with a sangoma who told them that it was in fact true that Ntombi and the Nkosi family were in fact envious of them and they had solicited dark forces to bring about bad luck on that family. The sangoma even told them who the Nkosi's had consulted with and which muti they had used to blacken out their fortunes. According to the sangoma, the Nkosi's had burned the sheath of a monkey's gall bladder and some bank notes in a hollowed out turtle shell and then buried the ash along with the shell, turned upside down, in the veld where no one would ever discover them. The effect of that, supposedly, was to make sure that their fortunes would just evaporate and because it was in a turtle shell, the bad luck would to stay with them forever and for generations to come. Again the news of that consultation soon spread like a rampant veldfire through the village and Ntombi and her family were greatly ostracized. The superstitions got to the point that if anyone had any ill fortune, it was attributed to Ntombi, her babblings and her witchcraft. Any and all sangomas in the oSizweni area had heard about Ntombi and the Nkosi's were not too keen in the solicitation of sangomas, as matter of fact baba Nkosi forbade them even mentioning sangomas in his house; he firmly believed in the Bible and to him the ancestral ways of the sangomas and the ancestors themselves were heathen and a dying way of life. He often said that he could not understand how using some grounded up tree bark or plant could cause good fortunes on one person or trigger bad fortunes to another; to him it was all a way for those charlatans to make money or increase their livestock from the gullible villagers. The missionary taught him how to pray, to repudiate all other forms of worship and spiritual practices and he told him to believe solely in the word of God and being a farm labourer with limited literacy, he could not really interrogate the scripture to get the full message for himself; he had to accept what he was being told as fact. Nonetheless, the family still suffered a lot of persecution from the other villagers and that took its toll on them, to the point that Ntombi started believing that she was actually a witch because she could predict all sort of bad things that would happen in the future. Slowly she drifted away from her siblings and then from her parents and began shutting herself out from the family circle and as a growing young woman she still longed for motherly love and someone whom she could talk to and share her feelings with. However, seeing that she was losing the connection with her own family, she gradually formed a new bond with one of her mother's friends, Ma-Nkabinde, a neighbour who in her sense of being neighbourly, listened to the young girl as she tried very hard to make sense of what was going on in the young girl's head and life. Ntombi felt that she could trust and confide in her partly because of the surrogacy that existed in the village and the way of life during those times; it was the time when communal rights weren't bogged down with individual rights. The children of the village were taught that every adult was to be treated with the same respect that they would treat their own parents and that also meant that each and every adult in the village was responsible for the discipline of every child. This discipline usually meant a whipping, first from the supposedly aggrieved adult and then later from the child's parents when they came back from the fields. The transgressions included refusal to run an errand, back chatting or looking into an adult's eyes whilst being talked to and the more serious transgressions were ones where culture had been compromised. It was the old way, a way that a lot of modern urban folk pined for and felt that if it had prevailed, it would have helped curtail the current youth plagues that fester amongst the modern society such as drugs or teenage pregnancies and young violent, drug fuelled gangs. According to these same modern urbanised respectable folks, the world started falling apart when the new democracy and its dang fangled constitution came into being and kids got their rights.

Ntombi was in desperate need for someone to help her understand what was going on because she wasn't getting any answers
from her mother or aunts or anyone in her family for that matter, so she bore her soul to Ma-Nkabinde and she in turn tried her
utmost to explain what was happening to Ntombi but realised
that she had bitten off more than she could chew. Ma-Nkabinde
was a widow and she knew what it was like to be cast out by society and for years she was the victim of gossip and stinging
rumours in her own village until she packed her bags and re-
located to oSizweni. She could relate to the loneliness, confusion and dysfunction that that type of societal exclusion led to,
so Ma-Nkabinde decided that the best thing that she could do
was to take Ntombi away for a while so that she could have a
chance to recoup. Ma-Nkabinde didn't have to do much in order
to convince the young girl or her mother to let her accompany
her to some relatives; she said it would do Ntombi good to get
away from the entire natter that had overshadowed her and the
Nkosis. Baba Nkosi was not so keen but he finally relented and
day after the schools closed, they left for Isandlwana, the village
where Ma-Nkabinde was born. The journey took about a day
and a half of travelling catching lifts on tractors and bakkies and
walking through the luscious velvety green valleys and velds of
Natal; they were offered food and shelter for the evening by one
of the farmstead's families that they had cut through along the
way and the in the mid-morning after they had been well rested
and given food for the rest of the journey. Ntombi kept reflecting upon the hospitability of their hosts and realised why and
how important the teaching that her own parents had been
preaching and practising was about accepting guests and stran-
gers into their home with open arms. She felt a great sense of
connection and belonging, not only to their hosts but to humanity as well, a feeling that had she been harshly detached
from since she had surrendered to the anger, bitterness and hatred that had welled up inside her. For those few hours, she felt

like a young girl again as she played with their host's daughters and helped them in doing their chores of getting water from the river and as they helped their mother prepare and cook supper and again in the morning when they cleaned the yard and prepared a meal for the rest of the trip for Ntombi and Ma-Nkabinde. They finally reached Isandlwana at dusk. It's situated about fifteen kilometres east of Rorke's Drift and it's a decorous village, pretty similar to oSizweni and comprised of a close knit community of vastly dispersed huts and kraals but the stark difference were the fat, seemingly well nourished livestock that were lazily roaming about unattended. When Ntombi commented to Ma-Nkabinde about them, she was quickly informed that about a third belonged to the chief and the rest belonged to the family they had come to visit. She also added that the area boasted a great deal of colonial history of how the British under Lord Chelmsford suffered a humiliating defeat. Children and adults alike greeted the two visitors with such warmth and that Ntombi began to feel the peace that Ma-Nkabinde was telling her about and every once in a while she would stop and chat with a rustic but would cut the welcoming pleasantries because they needed to get to Sibiya's house before it got too dark.

Bab' Sibiya's house was on the slope at the end of the village, even on the final approach to its footpath, the house remained concealed and in the darkness of night it was almost impossible to locate. The footpath was winding downwards and only on the second curve would the house reveal itself to its visitors, first would be the thatch of the roof and then the long poles at the gates. On the end of each of the long poles at the gate were horned dried out skulls. Skulls at a gate?!? That was the equivalent of a modern day neon sign and that sign read: sangoma. The sight stirred uneasiness in Ntombi, her mind topped up with questions and at the same time she tried to convince herself that they hadn't reached their final destination. Her eyes darted about in the creeping dark, between the gate and Ma-Nkabinde as she miserably waited for Ma-Nkabinde's next step or comforting words at least. When Ma-Nkabinde's movement made the direction clear, she took a hesitant step and as she placed her foot inside the yard, a sharp, cold westerly breeze arose and she froze whilst the mysterious wind snaked itself around her as if someone had told her to stand still while she was being given the once over. Her heart raced and she began to sweat, her eyes locked onto Ma-Nkabinde who walked on, oblivious to what was happening behind her. She tried to call out to the motherly woman but as soon as she opened her mouth to summon her, the wind sounded like it was whispering to her to shush and remain perfectly still. It daubed itself around her from her feet up and it felt cold and clammy and she was helpless to act and even if she could react, she had no idea what she would or could do. With that, the wind continued with its venture and as it moved up, it felt like it had let itself into her as she then felt the same cold clamminess inside her, first at the base of her stomach, almost squeezing her like she had a sudden case of menstrual pains and then it moved higher to her solar plexus where she could feel herself running out of breath and to her thumping heart, where it felt like it was being pierced with a multitude of sharp pins. Her eyes turned red as they welled up with tears but not tears of pain or wanting to cry but rather an involuntary reflex of her body reacting to the breath that was being squeezed out of her, her head felt like it was going to explode from the excessive rush of blood flowing towards her forehead. She could barely focus on the ground in front of her as she commanded her body to move but her feet felt as heavy as the big cast iron pots that they used for the big family gatherings. Eventually, she found her voice and with all the energy she had left, she let loose her vocal chords and all that came out was a shallow, dwindling and fading: 'Maaaaaa...'

'Kade ngikumele!' (I've been waiting for you), said a gruff voice which had undertones of a woman and a child's voice all in one,

'Ungubane wena?' (Who are you?), she dared ask and shocked

that her speech was resolute unlike a moment earlier when she could not even call out to Ma-Nkabinde,

'Uwazi kahle kuthi ngiwubani mina!' (You know very well who I am), the voice rasped, 'angithi ngehlele nawe yonke impilo yakho, ngibonisa zonke lezintho ozibonayo' (I've been living with you all your life showing you all the things that you've been seeing),

'Kuthi ungibiza bani, akubalelekanga; o kumcokwa ukuthi uwazi kuthi ozongi sebenzela ngaphandle ko ku ngabaza, ozowenzo loku engitjela kona, gu ngase njalo, kuningi o kuza mosakala!' (who you call me is irrelevant, what is important to know is that you will serve me without hesitation, you will do as I say, failing which there will be consequences!), the voice asserted and as it did so, she felt her stomach hollowing out and filling with a terrible fear, worse than what she had felt while the wind was examining and probing her. Ntombi shot up and landed screaming in the arms of Ma-Nkabinde, who was sitting alongside her on a grassmat. She was wet from sweat and hyperventilating;

'Shhh...Shhh... Zonke izintho zizo lunga, sisi; thula ngane yam. Sesifike ekugcineni kwo hambo lwethu!' (Shhh...Shhh... Everything will be alright, dear; be still my child. We've come to the end of our journey!') Ma-Nkabinde lulled Ntombi.

While she rested her head on Ma-Nkabinde's bosom, catching her breath, she began consuming her surroundings. They were in a candle lit room, heavily drenched in smoke which seemed to be coming from a receptacle on the ground on her left. She could barely make out the figure that was squatting behind smoke and blowing the cinders to produce more of the choking smoke, it smelt like grass but it was much harsher on the nose than ordinary veld grass burning. The room began to spin around and she could once again barely focus on the myriad of animal skins, bottles and tins that filled the room. To try keep her composure, she made every effort to focus on the drum-beats that were coming from outside, accompanied by young maidens' voices chanting and singing in unison to the drums and clapping hands. The smoke became thicker and then a voice grunted as if the person was trying to catch their breath or belching backwards, it was a deeply disturbing sound and one that she had never heard before and if it was not for the occasional: 'Iii-yo!! Yebo makhosi!!' (Iii-yo!! Yes, Oh great ones!!), she would have thought that some large wild animal had strayed into the hut and was lurking behind the smoke and responding to the call of the drum and the maidens. She was dazed and petrified and really wished that her mother was there to take her away from all that surrealism but all she had was her surrogate mother Ma-Nkabinde who kept assuring her that everything was fine and that it would all be over soon and she should relax and not try to struggle.

The drumming became stronger and more monotonous like it was flat lining in her brain and soon she felt that she was withdrawing into her mind like she was being lulled. Her consciousness withdrew and she saw herself retreating in her mind to some safe place within her mind, she could see her body being taken over by another being, one that she could not clearly identify as being human or animal in nature but she felt that she knew this being, she was not entirely scared of it but just stunned by the whole activity. Shortly after the transference of the body to this new being, she partially passed out, catching glimpses of the activities that were taking place all around the yard. At some point she was hovering above the whole yard and even though it was at night, she could see every living creature that breathed that was in her sphere of sight, anything that moved she could see it and if it made contact with her eyes, it would remain trapped in her gaze until she let it go. In another vision, she saw herself walking in a very large compacted crowd and all the beings were in hooded robes and all but one had the hoods over their bowed heads. She moved towards the unhooded being but before she could touch them to ask where she was and what was happening there, the drumming became more apparent and she turned focus towards it. She was being led out of the candlelit, smoky hut to a chanting, screaming and swooning crowd that had gathered outside but the way she so groggy; she could barely make out the faces. She was taken to the centre of the circle and the clapping of the hands and the drum played out in the background while in the foreground an array of snorting, grunting and exclamatory gasping became louder; at first it sounded like it was coming from the crowd and she tried to follow it, just so that she could find something to focus on and fully regain her consciousness but the more she listened, the more she realised that it was coming from her but she was sure that she was not making the noises.

'Vukani Makhosi! Sinilalele Makhosi amakhulu!' (Wake up Great Ones! We are listening oh Great Ones!), a deep feminine voice rasped over the lowered chants, clapping and drumbeats. A heavy set woman dressed in a faded red cloth underneath a leopard skin loincloth was bowed down, clapping and cupping her hands as she spoke towards Ntombi, the homemade animal rattles on her wrists and ankles crackled like the fire next to her whenever she moved. She was accessorised with pelts; a mongoose was slung over her left shoulder, partially covering her breast and an unidentifiable yet moderately hard skin slung over her right shoulder. The two hides criss-crossed over her breastplate and on her neck was an assortment of necklaces that hung as if their weight were the ones causing her to bow.

'Sinilethele umhlatshelo Makhosi! Sinilethele ithwasa Makhosi!' (We have brought you a sacrifice Great One! We have brought you an apprentice Great One!), she rasped on. At some point the voice had a certain familiarity to Ntombi but she could not be certain because in her head there was a cacophony between the drums, the clapping hands, the chanting, the prancing feet with rattles and the voices of the woman bearing

149

gifts and the great one telling this strange woman, in a ancient foreign dialect, what was expected of them, especially with Ntombi. The woman's face rose up and when her eyes locked with her possessor's she immediately recognised her: it was Ma-Nkabinde. She would never have identified her under normal circumstance because beneath that entire garb was an ashen body with a braided head of hair. Ntombi had never seen Ma-Nkabinde without any form of headwear, especially her doek or turban.

Ntombi screams inside could not be heard by anyone except her and her possessor and as they took her body towards the sacrificial animal, she fought and kicked but her body was not responding to any of the commands to resist. She persisted in fighting off the crowd and finally the sound of her parents' voices and her father's firm grip on her writhing body brought her about her senses. She was back in her house, completely drenched in sweat and thirsty. Her mother stood two steps behind her father with her hand on her chest, completely over-whelmed by her daughter's behaviour. When things had calmed down a bit but having failed to get a word out of their daughter, she insisted that Ntombi should take the holiday with Ma-Nkabinde.

THE MAN

There was more to Judas than what I thought I knew a whole lot more. Judas had an evil and corrupt mind and he was hiding it all under the guise of being a church leader. He had gathered himself a strong following and his knowledge and interpretation of the Bible kept the congregants mesmerised. It was, in part, the trait that he had inherited from his grandmother, hers being able to reduce people to a whimper with a gaze, he had worked on that and upgraded it to captivate and hypnotise an audience and it worked. His charm worked wonders, especially on those that needed salvation because he portrayed himself to them to be righteous and without blemish and what was even more frightening was that he knew people's fears and especially their needs.

For starters when he recruited me, he knew what my problems were in KZN and he mentioned how in the project that he was working on we would use nepotism in our favour because unlike the corporates, there would be no board or stakeholders to account to. He made it clear that we could give preference to those we wanted to employ such as our own family, church members, pretty much anyone we preferred to employ. He made it sound so honourable that we would be giving them the opportunity to earn a salary and I was so taken by that and we did do that. We gathered a bunch of CV's, mostly from his congregation and I did the interviews, he had final say on the appointments and I did the training and by the end of May 2009, we were operationally ready as far as the staff was concerned. I fell for his charms and jelly words and carried out his plan without any glitches. During August, I was dispatched to find business outside the airport and when I came back in November some of the guys that we had started off with had left and the ones that remained were morose and when I did my rounds to find out why the sudden sullen mood, talks came out that Judas was telling the staff from his church to tithe ten percent of their salary, where of course he was the head. Tithing has been a religious practise for centuries and I expected that these kids knew that, especially in their church and with that I thought that those kids were being unfair on the man because he was just following religious teachings and I began dismissing it all as calumnious talk. However, the talks persisted and when I overheard him talking to one of the managers, who was his cousin and another guest that they too, ought to compel the kids that worked there but were in their churches to do the same, I backtracked and inquired from the other kids and a manger that were not in his church and the stories held. I then calculated and found that from the average salary of R3 200, with fifty three of the seventy-two staff belonging to his church at a tithe of R320 per staff, it meant he was getting close to R17 000 per month, just from his staff. The sad part of it all was that if they said that they were unable to tithe or unable to get to church on a Sunday that they were off, he threatened to dismiss them from his company and because they feared him and in order to remain employed, they had to pay his church at the end of the month. Even with that knowledge, at first I didn't want to believe that that was the type of man he was, I convinced myself that I knew him and I knew him to be reverent and compassionate and as far as those kids were concerned, I felt that they were being calumnious. I had known him and seen him to be a slave master as a boss but as a person, he was nothing like that. I could bring myself to believe that he was capable of siphoning money from the till, it was after all his money and if he and Ashwipe had decided that they want to swindle the airports authority in order to maximise the profits, there was little I could do but for him to use religion and church in that manner was something that I could not bring myself to believe about Judas. He was a man of the cloth and an honourable man as far as religion was concerned, he wasn't one of those fly-by-night televangelist priests.

I was disillusioned by all that I had heard and I figured that I should approach him on the matter but I didn't want to cause any animosity between him and his congregants and an opportunity availed itself for me to highlight him of the concerns through a discussion with his wife but when she echoed her husband's sentiments, my heart sank. I felt that I had betrayed those kids; it felt like I had forced them to join the company so that they could be manipulated by their Bishop and that I had known of his plan all along. I could not rationalise which was the lesser of the two evils; the gambling company, which I had left on the principle that I felt that I was persuading people to give us whatever little hard earned cash they had or the wrapping company where my mentor and coach was proving to be a tyrant. The little bit of respect that I had left for my friend waned even further and it was not long after that that I tendered my resignation because I loathed him as the unscrupulous business man that he had shown himself to be and I rejected him as a coach and mentor.

Even though Judas was the easiest to get to because I already had his all the information about him and his operations - passwords, spreadsheets, banking details, suppliers, customer database. I had medical information about him and his entire family, from his youngest and most beloved daughter, Palesa to his dearest wife and ex-wife and even his wife's ex-husband. The plan was not as easily executable as it might have seemed about him and his operations - passwords, spreadsheets, banking details, suppliers, and customer database. Somewhere in the recesses of my mind, I realised that I still cared for the bugger, I still had feelings for him; we were as close as brothers and I had trusted him and he had also trusted me and for what our relationships, as colleagues and as friends, had been worth, I was in conflict about causing him the magnanimous pain that I had wanted to. At one point I justified it t myself that he started it first but then would correct myself by telling myself that two wrongs don't make a right. My conscience would hound me and remind me of all the teachings that I had received; 'Love thy neighbour' and all that and 'You are have to be the better and bigger man' but in honesty, I wasn't doubting all those sensible words; I just wanted something more: an eye for an eye and I wanted it immediately. I knew that the world would get back at him but I still wanted to and was willing to get my hands dirty and see the look on his face as his world came crumbling in all around him. Yes; that was it, that's the justice I was looking for; seeing him in pain after he had thought that I was down and out. I wanted to show him that I was a fighter and that I could take it as good as he and Ashwipe gave it but would they be able to take it just as well or as graciously. I felt that he deserved my dose of justice because I felt that he sat idly by as Ashwiphe plotted and pulled of a devious plan to have me incarcerated. He was supposed to defend me as I would have, if I were in his shoes. Besides, had I not meted out enough justice by handing over all that I knew to Tobey and his henchmen? The information that I had given them was enough for Judas and Ashwipe to halt their operation or at least change the way they had been doing business and the legal costs in defending their villainous deeds were far more than what we had contracted to. Justice? Had I not received justice even if it was not the justice that I had had in mind? Judas and Ashwipe had paid even more for their transgressions against me and the ninth commandment. I think I just wanted to play God and be their judge, jury and especially their executioner but then would that have made me a better person or really vindicated me. Did I really need vindication? From what? From whom? I did not commit any crime that warranted me to seek vindication. Moloi and all those arresting officers knew that I was not a criminal, Woolbury and Melanie, the prosecutors refused to believe that I was a drug peddler, Molwedi was convinced that I was not a dealer, Tobey, Alwyn, Surge and Marius definitely knew that I was being set up, my family was aghast when they heard of the arrest, more so the reasons for the arrest; so whose vindication did I desperately seek? God? Not a chance in hell, He knew that this crucifixion was fictitious and that the nails would not even pierce my skin. My vindictiveness was purely human and not even fully based on the laws of self preservation; I just wanted to prove that I had a fight in me. I wanted to prove to Nthabi and those around me that I was not a wimp but in actual fact they did not even ask that of me; they just wanted me to stand up and dust myself off and carry on, to face the oncoming challenges and be the person, the son, the brother, the uncle, the father and the husband that they knew and loved and supported so much.

My self inflicted fears made me believe that I would have been a coward for not facing up to these bullies but neither Nthabi nor the rest of the family saw me as a lesser man for not dealing with Judas and his cohorts in the old fashioned ghetto manner. As a matter of fact she and the rest of the family were worried that I might actually do just that or worse and in as much as they watched most of my moods and moves, I could see that they were glad that I didn't pick up a gun and go Rambo on Judas; they expected it and waited with abated breath for it but they were relieved each night when they heard that I had turned in for the night peacefully, or so they thought. In reality, I had been skulking about and had gotten rather good at it and gathering intel for my master plan; my plan for revenge, mayhem and justice; my brand of justice the Charles Bronson way. God knows that I wanted to and with all that I had acquired; I was only moments away from going through with it but to what avail? Would I have achieved the inner peace that I so desperately wanted or would I have opened up a new lifestyle, a life where I would have to look over my shoulder for the rest of my life? What would I have taught my sons? I hope and believe that through this I would have taught them that the pen is truly mightier than the sword and that intellect is probably one of their greatest weapons in any fight and challenge that they will face. However, I want to believe that more than anything, faith and belief in God has been my greatest arsenal. I may have doubted at times and had little faith at times but that little that I had got me through those difficult and trying times and paramount to that, the lessons which I learnt during those tribulations will be lessons that will help me keep my head held up high and be able to see danger from afar.

THE PASTILLE

Judas and Ashwiphe, as well as all those that have done me in-justice, not only during this incidence but in others as well, let me share something with you; you are the failures. Yes! You failed dismally at annihilating my spirit and simply because you didn't create me; God did. I don't, never have and never will belong to you or anyone in this earth; not even my mother and father who bore me own me, so who do you think you are to try something as futile as what you did. You need more power than money and your incongruous desires to destroy a person. What you have all proved to me is that I am a very powerful person; I'm the conscience that you are avoiding and one word from me sends you into a tremor and you fear that I can do more damage to you and your avaricious desires and self-worth than what all your enemies could do to you collectively. You have shown me your fears, your flaws and all your malignant concerns. I am con-vinced that if you had focused all that energy on working on your short comings rather than trying to paint a bull's eye on my forehead, you would have achieved so much more than what you currently have or had; I know that because the energy it took me to put my scheme together was so draining. Let me as-sure you that from the onset, I was never your problem, the truth was; you did not like the notion of having to face the truth or be told where you had gone off the rails so in some fleeting and feeble moment you averted that denial and opted to see me as the problem and by so doing you then convinced yourselves that I had to be dealt with. Let's just reflect on the budget of that exercise. How many sleepless nights did you have thinking of how to discredit me or to get rid of me? How much did the phony raid cost you? How much was it to get the guys that were supposed to hijack me? How much was the judge that covered the civil suit? How much did the labour department people cost you? How much did the CCMA people cost you? Personally I think you could have a saved a penny or two with the labour department, their incompetence would have done the job for you. Thus far it seems that all you have managed to do was corrupt more and more people and still I stand without so much as a hair on my head touched. Maybe I'm just like Job, Satan did his bit to get him to curse God but in everything that he tried, that man stood firm in his belief in God. So if some old Jewish guy could beat the devil like that, what could stop me from pummeling you at the same game; you, just like me, are only human; no matter how much you may act like a tin god; you're are far from being a deity of any sort. My death at your hands would only prove one thing: that I fear you and not God. Take comfort in the fact that you're not the first one to attempt to relieve me of my liberty or my right to life and that like the ones that have tried before you, you share a common achievement: failure.

On the flipside of the coin, I do want to thank you but don't think that this note of gratitude comes with complete forgiveness; oh no! I'm still some distance from forgiving you for the pain that I felt but I'll get there soon; maybe sooner than you or I can imagine. What do I have to thank you for? Your cheating me has brought me closer to God and my family; something that probably would have taken longer to accomplish, make no mistake we were close but you just brought us closer, much closer. I also have to thank you for releasing me of the trappings of corporate slavery, being a lackey and the various social and economic maladies that I had been caught up in. You see, your band of marauders just got me to be more of a home body; I partied less, gave up smoking and drinking completely (and you know how much of a problem that had become for me) and really focused on my wife and kids and rekindled with my creative side, hence all this writing. Once again, I would have had to wait until I had reached retirement age to start on my first book but now thanks to you and Ashwiphe, I can afford to raise my kids myself - no nanny, just me, which means that I can get to do all the things that most parents would really like to do with their kids: walk in the park, do homework with them, instill my values into them, teach them how to cook and help them grow up to be honest men with integrity. You may have taken away a formal salary from me but you allowed to get a real job; a job that God gives us all as parents. How about you? Who is watching over your kids? Did you get to see them take their first steps or utter their first words or was it all up to their nanny or your wives or mistresses? Did you just get to hear about their achievements at school or were you there every single day. Before all this mess, I really thought that a man's job was to bring home the pound of flesh but through your greed and all that rot, I've learnt that I have not been rendered impotent by being a stay home dad. In one way you did kill me; you killed off the that beast that you had spawned all those years back during our tenure at the airline and out of its ashes a phoenix is rising but even at that don't get megalomania and think that all this re-birth was your doing; sorry mate that honour belongs to God, Nthabi and my family. You get credit for the turning point and no further and still at that not all the credit. From here on in, if things were to go south then it would really be all my doing and entirely my fault but with all the hardships that you have allowed me to experience, I am cocksure that I have a learnt enough to keep me away from the likes of you and your ilk. Did I thank you for the stronger marriage that I have with Nthabi; no? Well I suppose that that prayer ritual that you lead where you had us break candles, cross our arms and do all sorts of irrational things and then finally bury them in the veld didn't go according to plan but then it's ok; you'll learn to accept disappointment when your plans don't go accordingly; I did. I suppose the handing over of the candles by crossing our arms was a way to get us to swap roles whereby I would be emasculated but instead it has gotten me to be more sensitive to my wife's emotions, needs and desires. For starters, I get the wonderful opportunity to pack her lunch when she goes to work and I even get to pot in a personalised note on a napkin for her - she says it beats the sms because the note is in my hand writing. When she gets home, I'm not too tired to listen to her about how her day was and to give her advise on how to deal with the corporate types. I managed to teach her how to drive and now she drives like a grand prix driver, confidently and even better than I do. Even better than anything; I am debt free. Yep! I owe no one nothing, not a cent; even if I do thanks to you and your corrupt ways, I can't afford to pay them because I've been blacklisted and you know what, it doesn't bother us. No taxman, no debt collectors, no bills filling up our post box and no fear of private numbers on our cell phones. Go on call me from an unidentified number and you'll hear for yourself; you'll hear the sweet sound of liberation, liberation that even the ANC couldn't deliver on; sheer and utter emancipation. I must admit though there were times when I thought I would not make it through without all those bells and whistles that I had been accustomed to but then again kudos to God for helping us through it all. Man, you're a disaster; I remember when I used to get knots in my stomach when I would pick my phone up and see your number on the screen and start wondering what I had done wrong and how long I'd be in the dog box for; well it was you and the other fella from the gambling joint that used to make me feel that way. Now if either one of you were to call, instead of a whimpering and shaky 'Hello!?!' You'd probably get a 'Ufanani?' ('What do you want?). That's if I chose to take your call and again if I still have your numbers. You don't have power over me anymore and that was wrong in the first place, in retrospect I realise that I shouldn't have given you two so much respect and loyalty. I gave you more than you deserved but then that's all in past and 'Yippee' for that.

In as much as I have found this to be very therapeutic and refreshing, I have a diaper to go change and supper to prepare for my family, studying to help with and the day's adventures to listen to, so take care and when your demons come knocking, well I'm sure you'll be able to handle them; alternatively go ghetto on their asses.

Peace.

AUTHOR'S BIOGRAPHY

Mathews Nkoboli Lehlongwane is the fifth child and only son of Mathews Sakaria Lehlongwane and Martha Tshigoane Lehlongwane. He was fortunate to attend school at De La Salle Holy Cross College, a Catholic school in the Northern suburbs of Johannesburg during the heavy and oppressive apartheid era of South Africa.

Thokozani Cinema, the family business was established in 1980 by Mathews S Lehlongwane and it was only natural that he got incorporated into the operation from an early age. During weekends and holidays, along with his siblings, he would work in the various departments, such as ushering, the refreshment kiosks, ticket sales and the projection room; learning and gaining functional and soft skills.

By 1991, his responsibilities had increased to the point that he was managing the complex operationally and assisting administratively. By then the complex, consisted of two cinemas, a video library and ice cream factory, with a staff compliment of 30. His duties included having to deal with customer queries, human resources, liaising with the various movie and video distribution companies, including Ster Kinekor, United International Pictures, Nu Metro and Concorde Films. He also received on the job technical training for Cinemeccanica 35mm projectors and VCR's, both Betamax and VHS.

In 1992 an opportunity to explore the retail industry came available through Woolworths, Eastgate. He joined the ranks of casual temps, with the intention of understanding customer care and quality service delivery as a front liner. He worked week-ends and holidays until February 1993. By the time he left, he had worked on the floor as a sales assistant, as a cashier, as his knowledge increased and he proved his worth to the company, he was moved to more challenging positions. His final move was to the level of a PPC (Pay Point Check), which is the equivalent of an assistant supervisor.

He returned to Thokozani on a full time basis in 1995 and in 1997, when the business expanded and it was then when he was tasked with heading up the ice cream factory. This entailed having to be trained in the manufacturing of a Brazilian product locally and the distribution thereof.

He joined South African Airways in 1999, as a customer service agent in the passenger handling department. It was here under the mentorship of Mrs. Anisha Archary, the then Vice President of Global Passenger Services that he was developed into a team leader and got appointed to the position in 2001. He was further trained and developed through a developmental manager program, under the leadership of Mrs. Siza Mzimela and appointed as a duty manager in 2002. The position had him leading and managing six departments, viz. arrivals, check-in, boarding gates, ticket sales, transit desk and aircraft control centre (an irregular operations centre). This all came with managing the budget and training for each department.

In 2004, he was given the opportunity to manage South African Airways' client airlines department; which is the department that offers ground handling services for other airlines. This entailed liaison with the various station manager of the airlines that use SAA's services and ensuring that they receive consummate service for their arrival and departing passengers.

During 2005, he joined SAA's Customer Service department as

the senior manager for Service Recovery. Though this department's primary function is service recovery, it is also an important participant in ensuring that service gaps are averted at the customer touch points. Through the service recovery department, it became easier to suggest and source the relevant training required for the various departments.

In the beginning of 2006, he joined Mrs. Mzimela at South African Express Airways as a Senior Manager for Customer Service, Baggage Claims and Airport Operations. The customer service and baggage claims portfolios required the revising and implementation of procedures and policies. The airport operations needed the management of service level agreements and liaison with all the outstations where SA Express flew in and out of within the borders of South Africa and in the neighbouring countries.

2007 brought about an opportunity to take on Cargo Sales for SA Express Airways and once again it was a venture that required starting up and heading the department.

In 2008, he was approached by Mr. John Copelyn of Hoskens Consolidated Investments to join one of their subsidiaries: Vukani Gaming Corporation as a General Manager for the Kwa-Zulu Natal provincial office. This was for Limited Pay-out Machines in the gaming (gambling) industry. The focus was set on customer service.

In mid-2009, he joined Urban Innovative Management Services in the capacity of Operations Director. This was to establish an operations department for their baggage wrapping and storage services at O.R Tambo International Airport.

Though his professional life has been illustrious, he always emphasizes that his greatest pleasures and most memorable moments are in his personal life; from the childhood memories of numerous family trips to marriage to the birth of each of his children.

One of his greatest joys is spirituality and the path he has followed to reach the level of understanding that he has.

www.ingramcontent.com/pod-product-compliance
Lightning Source LLC
Chambersburg PA
CBHW021054130626
46552CB00005B/2092